NOBODY'S FAMILY

NOBODY'S FAMILY

by Anne Snyder
illustrated by Diane de Groat

HOLT, RINEHART AND WINSTON

New York

Published simultaneously in Canada by Holt, Rinehart
and Winston of Canada, Limited.

Snyder, Anne.
Nobody's family.
SUMMARY: When they accidentally become stowaways
on a private boat, three homeless children, a dog, and
a rooster change a number of lives.
[1.   Orphans—Fiction]   I.   De Groat, Diane, illus.
II.   Title.
PZ7.S68515No   [Fic]   74–10616
ISBN 0–03–013256–8

Printed in the United States of America
First Edition

To my husband, Louis Snyder
—A.S.

—D. deG.

NOBODY'S
FAMILY

I

For Maria Josefina Smith de Saldivar, a large wooden packing crate at the foot of the San Diego pier was home.

It was the same as all the other packing crates around it, except that this one had a kind of window cut on one side and an opening large enough to crawl through on the other. Above the opening, the crate was stamped, THIS SIDE UP.

Inside the packing crate, Maria dropped to her knees and gazed lovingly at the tiny statue of the Madonna standing on a small cardboard carton. The Madonna was chipped and faded but seemed especially beautiful this morning; today, she seemed to stare right back into Maria's eyes and smile.

"A good omen," thought Maria happily. She clasped her hands together and closed her eyes tightly.

"God bless Mama in Heaven," she whispered. "And

1

God bless Aunt Carmen and bring her back to get us." Maria paused. "God, we've been waiting for Aunt Carmen like she told us, but it's been an awful long time." Maria shuddered. "Maybe the *authorities* got her. Oh, God, please not that." She sighed. "We don't know what to do, God. We're waiting for a sign. Please give us a sign." Maria paused again, and then said, quickly, "Bless Pablo and Little David and Noches and Bandido and me. Thank you, Lord. Amen."

She opened her eyes and looked once again at her beloved Madonna. The Madonna was lovely, flanked on one side by a pickle jar filled with wild flowers and on the other with the stub of a candle. There was no question in Maria's mind that her prayers would be answered, God willing, in His own time, in His own way. She had only to wait. She had only to wait for a sign to tell her what to do. But waiting was hard . . . and sometimes scary.

Maria rose to her feet and picked her way carefully over the two small boys sleeping on the floor. One was her nine-year-old brother, Pablo. His eyelids fluttered and he turned on his side. Even in sleep, he seemed to be in motion. Like Maria, Pablo had dark skin and enormous black eyes.

The yellow-haired boy was Little David. Sometimes he said he was five, and sometimes he claimed to be six. Maria's guess was that he was four. She stooped down and covered him with the sweater he used as a blanket, which had fallen off. She remembered the first time she had seen him. Little David's young mother had offered Pablo a quarter to babysit him while she went off with a beach boy. When, by dark, she failed to return for the boy, Pablo had taken him home to the packing crate. Little David told them that his mother had often left him—once at a church with a note pinned to his shirt. That time, he waited until she turned the corner, and then he had followed her home. In the days after Little David came to them, the kids scoured the beach looking for the boy's mother. But they never saw her again and finally gave up the search. So Maria kept the boy, accepting him, as she did all things, as God's will. And for his part, Little David was perfectly content with his new little family.

Now, Maria turned away from the boys. She bent over almost double and got through the opening of the box to the outside. Before she could straighten up, the dog, Bandido, made a wild rush for her. Yipping excitedly, Bandido jumped up and down, licking Maria's legs, almost tripping her in his joy. His wiry hair tickled her legs, and she tried to scold him, but couldn't help laughing at the same time. "Down, Bandido," she said, as sternly as she could. "Be a good boy. You'll get your breakfast soon." But Bandido chose not to hear. Barking crazily, he jumped around her like a bouncing ball. Maria sighed and took him up in her arms.

She turned back to the packing box. Perched serenely atop the crate was Noches. "*Buenos días,* Noches," said Maria.

Unruffled, the shiny, black rooster blinked at Maria. Then he spread his wings and floated regally down to light at her feet.

Maria went to the "food cupboard," a small carton

placed upside down on top of a barrel. She took two half-eaten hot dogs and the remains of a hamburger out of a paper bag. She moistened the buns with water from a glass jar. "Breakfast, Noches," she said, as she put the buns down for the rooster. She watched Noches begin to peck daintily at the softened bread. Then she held the hot dogs and hamburger in her open hand while Bandido downed them in two quick swallows. "We're lucky there was a beach party last night," she said to Bandido. "Those people threw half their supper in the trash can." Bandido cocked his head and waited for more food. "That's all there is. Be glad you didn't have to eat like a rooster today."

Pablo, sleepy-eyed and blinking at the morning sun, came out of the packing box. "I'm starving!" He went to the food carton and rummaged around for something to eat.

"Me, too," said Little David, crawling out of the crate.

"Bananas," said Maria. "And crackers. And there's some orange drink left from last night."

Maria took the carton down and emptied it. Then she placed it on the sand and, like magic, it became a table. The boys sat down and waited for Maria to dole out the food. Pablo began to peel his overripe banana.

"Wait," said Maria. "First, grace."

The children clasped their hands and bowed their heads.

"We thank You for our daily bread," said Maria. "Amen."

4

"Amen," said Pablo, and took a big bite out of his banana.

"Little David?" prompted Maria.

"Me, too."

"Say it."

"Amen," said Little David.

"Now," said Maria, "we can eat."

The three children ate contentedly while Bandido circled impatiently around them waiting for a new day to begin.

2

After washing up in the public rest room on the beach, the kids started up the pier for the most important event of their day—to see how their ship was—to see if it was still there.

When the children first began to live in the crate, all the boats had been the same to them—some large, some small, all colorful, all *fantásticos*. But, then, one day, a new craft had sailed into the harbor and tied up to the pier. And in all her twelve years, Maria had never seen one like it.

This ship was like a proud queen and made all the others look like her lowly subjects. A long, sleek yawl, her hull whiter than the high clouds, her brass gleaming like the brilliant sun, the *St. Agnes* was perfection, like a sign from God.

And Maria had been certain, from the moment she saw her, that this ship was not just an ordinary boat.

This ship would play an important part in her life. She thought about it for days, and then it came to her: This was the ship that was destined to take them on a voyage, a quest, like the quest of the Holy Grail. The ship was ordained to take them on the search to find their long-lost American father, somehow, someway.

Halfway up the pier, the children stopped and took their favorite places opposite the *St. Agnes*; Maria and Pablo sat on the top rail, the rooster, Noches, beside them. Little David and Bandido sat below, on the warm, wooden planks of the pier.

"We board her again, tonight," whispered Pablo.

"Like always," Maria answered in a low voice.

"Maybe, they'll catch us," said Little David. "We'll go to jail."

"They won't catch us," said Pablo stoutly. "There's nobody on board at night."

"We gonna find your Papa tonight?" asked Little David.

"Shh . . . not so loud," said Maria. "Not yet. We have to chart our course. We have to plan. There's lots to learn about sailing a ship."

"Let's go tonight," urged Pablo. "I can sail her by the stars."

"Who told you that?"

"Ol' Cappy. You know. The old man who rents beach umbrellas. He used to always sail by the stars. He told me how. I can do it."

"He must be a hundred years old. People don't sail that way anymore," scoffed Maria. "They navigate . . . like in books."

8

"We don't need to navigate," said Pablo. "We can go by the stars."

"Not yet," said Maria firmly.

"What are we waiting for?"

"For a sign," said Maria.

"What sign?"

"I don't know," said Maria. "But I'll know it when it comes."

"You don't want to find Papa," Pablo said angrily. "You only want to chart courses and read books. I don't think you . . ."

"Shh . . ." said Maria. "Look."

On the deck of the *St. Agnes*, a man appeared from below. The children recognized him instantly. Red Hannigan was the "crew" of the ship and seemed to be as much a part of her as her sails. He had a thick, red beard and a booming voice. And although there were deep lines in his leathery face, he looked as strong and able as any of the workmen Maria had seen on the docks. The man came to the rail and dumped a bucket of water overboard. He was about to turn away when he noticed the kids. Scowling, he stared at them.

"He knows," Pablo whispered. "Let's get out of here." Pablo jumped down off the rail.

Maria sat still, her heart pounding. "Wait," she said. "Don't run. We're not doing anything."

"We never touched your ship . . . we're not doing anything!" Little David shouted.

"Be quiet!" Maria said.

Suddenly, the big man threw back his head and began to laugh, his red beard whipping in the breeze.

His laughter stopped abruptly when he noticed a black, chauffeured car glide to a stop on the pier beside the *St. Agnes*.

The driver got out of the car and opened the back door to let a white-haired woman step out.

"Well," smiled Red, "it's Mrs. Norton herself!"

The woman nodded to Red and turned back to the car. "We're here," she said curtly to someone inside. "Get out."

"I'll tell Jim you're here," said Red, and disappeared below.

Maria sighed in relief, glad Red's attention was no longer fixed on them. "It's all right," she said to the boys. "He knows nothing."

The three watched curiously as Mrs. Norton pulled a tall, skinny ten-year-old out of the car.

Maria, holding Noches, moved closer to get a better look. The boys and Bandido followed.

Ronnie Norton shook his grandmother's hand off his arm, and stood looking at her stonily.

"Your father will be surprised," Mrs. Norton said.

"Yeah," said the boy glumly.

"He'll be glad to see you."

"He doesn't want me," mumbled the boy.

"Of course he does."

"He never wanted me."

"Nonsense. He loves you," said Mrs. Norton. She started up the gangway, Ronnie trailing behind her.

Pablo ran his fingers over the shiny, black surface of the automobile, and whistled through his teeth. "Some car," he said.

10

The driver turned and scowled at the boy. "Don't touch, kid. Keep away." He loosened his tie and laid his cap on the hood of the car.

On deck, Jim Norton, the owner of the *St. Agnes*, came forward to greet his mother and son. He shook hands formally, first with Mrs. Norton, then with Ronnie.

Maria caught her breath. "That's what my Papa will look like," she whispered. "Tall, strong, light curly hair, flashing teeth . . . beautiful!" She moved forward to catch his words.

"Mother, it's good to see you. Hello, son."

"Hello," said Ronnie glumly.

"School's not out yet, is it? I didn't expect you," said Jim.

"You should have. I've written to you time after time. You know the trouble we've been having," said Mrs. Norton.

Jim frowned down at his son. "So he was kicked out of school. Put him in another school. What's the problem?"

Mrs. Norton looked squarely into her son's eyes. "Jim," she said, "I've done all I can. The boy needs his father . . . he needs you." She paused. "We're fast running out of schools."

Jim laughed shortly. "Come on, Mother, it's not that bad. Let's talk about it over a cup of coffee." He turned to Ronnie. "Mother and I have a few things to talk about. Why don't you look around?"

As Jim and his mother went below, Ronnie stood there looking lost and disappointed. After a moment, he walked up to the rail. Clenching both fists, he blinked his eyes to keep from crying. Then he saw Pablo at the car. Pablo waved.

"Hi," said Pablo.

"Hi," echoed Little David.

Ronnie glowered back at them.

"Come on," said Maria, "let's go."

"Hey, rich kid, can't you talk?" teased Pablo.

"Go away," said the driver. "Get lost."

"Pablo, come on," Maria said.

"Rich kid can't talk," Pablo taunted. He pulled back his lips with his fingers, and crossed his eyes.

"Buzz off, you weirdos!" shouted Ronnie. "Get away from my father's boat!"

"You heard what the boy said. Get away from his boat!" snarled the driver. He moved closer to Pablo. "Get going, kid . . . now! Move it!"

In one quick movement, Pablo snatched the driver's cap from the hood of the car and raced down the pier with Bandido at his heels.

Holding Noches like a football under one arm, Maria grabbed Little David's hand and ran. She could hear the driver's footsteps right behind them. "Run!" she yelled to Little David. "Run!"

When they made it to the foot of the pier, Maria saw Pablo disappear into the jungle of crates and barrels across the narrow stretch of sand. She looked over her shoulder. The driver had given up the chase, and was standing halfway down the pier waving his arms above his head.

12

"Thieves!" he shouted. "Little hoodlums! Come back here with my cap!"

Maria saw him turn back toward the car.

Dragging Little David along, she crossed the sand and made her way to the crate that was home—and safety. She pushed Little David and Noches into the opening and then plunged in herself.

Pablo was sprawled on the floor panting as hard as Bandido. He put the cap on his head backward and began laughing.

"He gone?" asked Little David fearfully.

Maria looked out. "Gone," she said. Then she saw the two blue-uniformed men walking toward the crate. "*Madre de Dios!*" she gasped.

"Police?" asked Pablo, instantly alert.

"Worse," Maria breathed, ducking back into the crate. She rolled her eyes heavenward and crossed herself. "The *authorities!*" she whispered.

3

The two officers were dressed alike. The gold shields pinned to the black straps across their visored caps identified them as U.S. customs inspectors.

In the crate, the children sat rigidly listening to the men's footsteps grow closer. Then the footsteps stopped.

"This the area?" said one of the men.

"Yeah. I want it cleaned up by noon tomorrow."

The first man whistled. "That's quite an order."

"I alerted maintenance. All you have to do is supervise." The man paused. "Oh, and keep your eyes open for some kids."

"What kids?" said the first man.

Maria held her breath.

"Mexican woman said she left two kids around here someplace. Boy and a girl."

Maria trembled.

"Since when are lost kids in my department?" said the first man.

"They're not. But the woman's being held for trial. Smuggled a wetback across the border in the trunk of her car."

"That's original," said the first man sarcastically.

"Yeah. Well, be on the lookout. Hate to think of little kids running around loose."

"Probably hitched a ride back to the Mexican side. Those kids are long gone by now . . . if there really were any kids in the first place," answered the first man.

"Well, keep your eyes open, just in case."

They started walking again, kicking tin cans aside as they went. Maria saw two pairs of men's feet pass the opening of the crate. Bandido began a low growl deep in his throat. Quickly, she drew the dog close.

The footsteps stopped abruptly. "Hear that?" said one of the men.

"What?"

"That sound . . . like a growl . . . or somebody moaning, maybe."

Maria patted Bandido until he lay down to be scratched.

There was silence for a long moment. Then: "I don't hear anything," the other man said. "Come on. Let's get to work."

"I could have sworn I heard something."

Little David pulled at Maria's sleeve. She put a finger to her lips, quieting the boy before he had a chance to say anything. The children sat breathlessly until the footsteps grew fainter, then faded away.

Maria peeked out of the opening. She could see the backs of the inspectors moving out of the area. Then she sat back down.

"They got Aunt Carmen," said Pablo, tightly.

"Shh, don't talk. Wait till they're gone."

Maria closed her eyes and tried to remember exactly what the men had said. ". . . held for trial . . . smuggling a wetback . . ."

Then Aunt Carmen was in jail. *That's* why she hadn't come back for them.

Aunt Carmen had taken care of Maria and Pablo ever since Mama had died. She was younger than Mama had been, and nearly as pretty. And she sang a lot. That was what Maria loved most about her—the way she sang. She knew hundreds of songs and had one for every occasion. When they were happy, she sang gay songs, funny songs, and made them all laugh. And when there was no work for Aunt Carmen, and they were hungry, she sang hymns that sounded like tender, gentle lullabys, and made them all feel good inside.

In the winter, the children went to school while their aunt worked. But in the summer, it was different. Summer was wonderful. Every morning, Aunt Carmen and the children left their one room in Tijuana, got into their old, battered car and crossed the border into San Diego, U.S.A., where Aunt Carmen worked. And all the way into San Diego, Aunt Carmen sang to the children.

Each day, she dropped the kids off at the beach and

went to do the housework in different U.S. ladies' homes; each evening, she came back to the beach to pick the children up. She had often told Maria, "If I don't come back on time, wait for me. Don't go away or I won't know where to find you. Wait . . . no matter what."

And Maria had promised, and she had kept her promise. But now Aunt Carmen was in jail. For how long? Maria didn't know what to do now. Should they hitch a ride back to Tijuana? Maria shook her head. No, Aunt Carmen was innocent of smuggling, or whatever the *authorities* had said. She would come back soon. They would wait on the beach no matter what.

"It's hot in here," said Little David. "I'm hot."

"One more minute," said Maria.

"I gotta go to work," said Pablo.

On hot days, when business was brisk, Ol' Cappy let Pablo hang around his umbrella stand and offer to help people carry their umbrellas to the sand. Sometimes he got tips, a nickel or a dime, sometimes even a quarter. One day, he had earned over a dollar, and the kids had a banquet of tacos and refried beans for supper.

Maria crawled out of the crate and looked around. The *authorities* were out of sight. "You can come out now," she said.

While Pablo worked at the umbrella stand on the boardwalk, Maria and Little David strolled on the public beach looking for someone to stare at. It was a game of which Little David was especially fond. The two walked, hand in hand, until Maria saw just the kind of family for which she was looking.

A pretty, black woman, surrounded by three small girls and a baby in a playpen nearby, was slicing a big, round cantaloupe. Maria and Little David stood a few feet away from their blanket and watched quietly.

The woman gave each of the girls a slice of the melon, and took one for herself. Then, noticing Maria and Little David, she smiled. Maria smiled back. The woman turned away and started to eat her melon. Maria, her own mouth watering, kept staring at her. Little David started toward the blanket, but Maria held him back. She kept on staring hard—as hard as she could. The woman turned and looked at her, and smiled again. Maria smiled back.

Then the woman said, "Want a piece?" Only now did Maria let go of Little David's hand.

"I do . . . I want a piece," said Little David, running to the edge of the blanket.

The woman gave Little David a large slice of cantaloupe and held another out to Maria. "Come on," she urged. "Have some. It's good."

Maria took the melon. "Thank you," she said. "Thank you very much."

"Wanna go make a sand castle?" said Little David to the small girls.

"Can we, Mama?" said one of the girls.

"We wanna make a sand castle," said another.

"Go ahead," said the mother. "But stay where I can see you."

18

Little David and the three girls went toward the water where the sand was damp and started digging. Maria sat on the hot sand next to the blanket.

"Don't you like to swim?" she said to the woman.

The woman laughed and turned to look at the sleeping baby in the playpen. "I love to swim," she said. "But I can't leave baby alone."

"I'll watch him for you. I'll watch all of them."

The woman looked closely into Maria's face. Then she said, "You sure you want to?"

"Sure," said Maria. "Go ahead. They'll be fine."

"You're an angel," the woman laughed. And she raced to the water's edge like a little girl herself.

4

Later in the day, Maria and Little David, stuffed with sandwiches, potato salad, and all the melon they could hold, made their way back to their packing crate. Pablo, still wearing the driver's cap, was sitting in front of the crate counting coins. He had earned seventy cents, and when Ol' Cappy had sent him to get a hamburger and a malt for lunch, the old man had treated him to the same. It had been a good day for all of them.

"Let's go to the ship," Pablo said, pocketing his money.

"It's not dark yet," said Maria.

"It's okay. I saw them all drive away. First the old lady and the driver. Then Red Hannigan and the owner in the jeep. The rich kid was with them."

"I don't know," said Maria. "We never go 'til it's dark. Maybe they'll come back."

20

"They never come back the same day."

Maria hesitated. Then Pablo went on, "You heard what the owner said. They probably went to put that dumb, rich kid in some dumb, rich school."

"We rich?" asked Little David.

"Sure we are," laughed Pablo. "We got a house, we got a ship, we got a rich American Papa." He turned to Maria. "Sooner we learn to sail that ship, sooner we'll find him."

"All right," agreed Maria. "Let's go."

Although no one had ever stopped them before, and they were pretty sure no one would stop them now, the children went through the usual elaborate procedures for boarding the *St. Agnes.*

First, Pablo and Bandido walked up the pier, Pablo whistling, pretending to be out for a casual evening stroll. He stopped beside the *St. Agnes*, looked around, then when he was sure no one was about, he lifted the driver's cap and signaled to Maria by scratching his head.

Maria, still on the sand, pushed Little David forward. "Go," she said.

Then Little David, holding Noches in both arms, ran to Pablo, who shooed him up the gangway. "Go below. Hurry!" Pablo told him.

Now it was Maria's turn. She sauntered up the pier, stopping once or twice to "admire" one of the boats. When she reached Pablo, he and Bandido raced up the gangway and disappeared below to join Little David and Noches. Maria looked up and down the pier. Satisfied that the coast was clear, she walked slowly up the

gangway, humming under her breath, as if she was there by invitation.

As always, Maria felt a thrilling sense of danger and excitement as she joined the others in the chart room. The childen looked at each other and grinned in satisfaction. They had done it again!

"What's in the plate?" asked Maria.

Since they first started their secret nighttime visits to the *St. Agnes*, there was always a plate of good things to eat on the galley table. The kids reasoned that, since it was left out, it was fair to eat it, but they never took anything.

In the beginning they had been tempted; there were so many beautiful things on the *St. Agnes*. Little David's favorite thing was the lovely, plush blanket on the bunk that felt like a foamy cloud. He never actually covered himself with it, but he spent long minutes running his hands over its softness and burying his face in its warmth. Pablo's interest lay in the overflowing food cupboard—he was always hungry. But Maria was most awed by the books. There seemed to be hundreds of them. And sometimes when she was finished studying the sailing books, she would pick up a novel and read until the others grew tired and fell asleep waiting for her to get ready to leave.

"Three cupcakes," said Pablo, bringing the plate to the chart-room table. He gave one cake to Little David and one to Maria. "And three pears."

"Good," said Maria. "Bring the books. Little David, you and Bandido and Noches are the lookouts. Go up on deck and tell us if you see anyone coming." Then she added seriously, "Look sharp."

Little David saluted. "Yes, sir, captain." He grabbed a pear off the plate, scooped up the rooster, and left the chart room with Bandido at his heels.

Pablo took some books off a shelf and brought them to the table.

"We'll go over our course from the beginning," said Maria. "First port of call . . . Ensenada."

"We did that already. A hundred times. We've gone over the first port of call, and the second port of call, and the third, and the fourth. When do we sail?"

"Soon. Maybe next week," said Maria, opening one of the books.

"Maria! Quick . . . come . . . hurry!" It was Little David's voice calling in alarm.

Pablo was first to reach the deck. "Maria! Look!" he shouted as Maria came to his side. "Our house!" He pointed toward the beach.

"Our house! It's going up to heaven!" said Little David.

The three watched open-mouthed as their packing-crate house, THIS SIDE UP on the bottom, dangled in the air at the end of a tall crane. The arm of the crane moved slowly toward a truck. Then their house was dumped, with a loud crash, onto the bed of the huge garbage truck.

"Holy smoke!" said Pablo.

"Holy smoke!" said Little David.

"*Madre de Dios!*" said Maria.

24

Maria and Pablo looked at each other in horror, then back to the activities on the beach. The crane was scooping up more crates and barrels while the two inspectors stood by and watched. One of them held something in his hand. And even from this distance, Maria could tell what it was—her beloved, beautiful Madonna. Pablo took his sister's hand as he noticed the tears form in her eyes.

Suddenly a taxi made a sharp swing onto the pier.

"It's them!" said Pablo. "The owner . . . Red . . . rich kid . . . they're coming back!" The kids stood motionless as the taxi rumbled toward them

Maria looked in panic from the taxi to the *authorities* on the beach. There was no place to run, no place to go. She looked wildly around the boat. "Hide! Quick!"

Pablo moved first. He dashed across the deck and unlatched a little door ahead of the forward cabin. "In here!"

The children dove into the deck locker, and Pablo shut the door behind them.

"The animals!" said Maria. "We forgot the animals!"

Pablo opened the little door, leaned out, and grabbed Noches. He held the door open. "In!" he ordered Bandido, and slammed the door shut after the dog.

Barely daring to breathe, the children sat in the tiny space in the pitch blackness with their knees touching their chins.

"Keep Bandido quiet," said Maria, wrapping her arms around Little David. "Don't make a sound," she warned the little boy.

They could hear the taxi come to a stop. Then they felt the motion of the boat as Jim, Red, and Ronnie came aboard. They could tell by the sounds that the three were going below. Then there was silence.

Little David began to whimper. "It's dark in here . . . I'm afraid. I wanna go . . . I want my Mama," he cried.

Maria held the boy tighter. "Don't cry . . . we'll be caught."

"We'll be caught . . . we'll go to jail . . . like Aunt Carmen," whined Little David.

"Shh . . ." said Maria. "Let me think."

The boat rocked gently as the children heard the muffled movements of those below.

"We'll wait 'til they leave. Then we'll get off," said Maria. "It'll be okay."

"What if they don't leave?" asked Pablo. "What if they sleep on board?"

For a moment, Maria didn't answer. Then she said, "We'll wait 'til they're asleep. Then we'll go."

"Let's go now . . . we can run for it . . . we can . . ."

Maria interrupted. "Quiet," she whispered, "they're coming back up."

"Ronnie, grab this rope." That was Red's voice. Then there was a long creaking sound and a dull thud.

For what seemed like hours, the children sat in their cramped quarters, their limbs aching, and listened to a jumble of muffled voices and confusing sounds.

Maria's arms were numb, and she could tell by the

sound of Little David's breathing that he was asleep. Suddenly there was dead silence.

"Pablo," whispered Maria.

"What?"

"Maybe they've gone to sleep."

"Yeah."

"We'll wait a little longer. Then we'll go."

"All right."

"You carry Noches. I'll take Little David," said Maria.

"Okay."

And then they heard it!

There was no mistaking the purr of the motor as the ship began to vibrate.

The children sat frozen as the *St. Agnes* moved out of the harbor and headed for the open sea!

5

"*Ay, caramba!*" moaned Pablo softly.

"*Dios, mío!*" breathed Maria.

The motion of the ship grew stronger, gently rocking the children in the darkness of the deck locker. They sat stiffly, no one daring to speak—hardly daring to move.

Then after what seemed a very long time, the motor stopped. Muffled voices, sounds of flapping sails being unfurled, and ropes being lashed were heard.

Then all that the children could hear was the slapping waves against the ship and squeaking, creaking sounds, like mice at play.

"Let's go overboard . . . *vámanos* . . . swim for shore," said Pablo.

"Little David . . . he can't swim." Maria shifted the sleeping boy in her arms.

For a moment, Pablo was quiet. Then he said, "We

could hold him up . . . between us . . . we'll make it."

"What about Noches . . . Bandido? Would you leave them here?"

"We can't do that."

"We can't hold them all up," said Maria.

"No," said Pablo.

"Pray," Maria said. "Pray hard." She rested her chin on Little David's head. She closed her eyes tightly and said a silent prayer.

"I got it," said Pablo.

"What?"

"We'll take the ship back to shore."

"That's crazy," said Maria.

"When they're asleep. We'll steer the ship back to shore, then get off. They'll never know."

"It won't work. We can't sail the ship."

"Sure we can. All those books you've been reading. We can do it," said Pablo.

"We can't," said Maria. "It's crazy."

"You were waiting for a sign. This is it."

"It's not," said Maria.

"How do you know?" Pablo said.

"I know."

"Okay," said Pablo. "We'll give ourselves up."

For a moment, there was silence, and all that could be heard was Little David's gentle snoring. Then Maria sighed. "That's all we can do."

"They'll call the *authorities.*"

Maria felt her stomach flip.

"They'll take us to jail," said Pablo.

30

"We'll take the ship back to shore," Maria said.

"Right," said Pablo. "Come on."

"Little David's asleep."

"He's good for all night. Leave him here with Bandido and Noches. We'll come back for them."

"Stay," Pablo said to Bandido. Then he crawled out of the deck locker. Maria put Little David down and slipped out beside her brother. Pablo closed the door. "Ready?" he said.

Maria took a deep breath. "Ready," she said.

The children looked all around them. They could see no lights—there was no moon. In a world made of black velvet, it was impossible to tell where the sky left off and the water began. A stiff wind came up and blew their hair back from their faces.

"Which way is shore?" asked Pablo.

"I don't know," said Maria. "We'll have to navigate. Let's go to the room of the charts . . . find the direction."

Holding hands, they felt their way down the companionway and into the chart room.

"Stand still," said Pablo, "I'll find the lamp."

"Wait. First close the curtains."

Maria could hear Pablo fumbling in the darkness. Then the little room was flooded with soft light from the swinging lamp overhead.

"Get the books," said Maria.

"Shh . . . I hear something."

"What?"

"That noise. Hear it?"

"Only the wind . . . the wind is coming up." Maria

held on to the table to keep her balance as the ship began to rock. "Don't waste time. Get the books."

Pablo brought the books and put them on the table. The ship lurched and the books went crashing to the floor. When Maria reached down to pick them up, the boat heaved and they slid, like live things, from under her hands. Pablo scrambled after them and put them back on the table.

Then they heard the voices.

"They're coming!" said Pablo.

"The light . . . turn off the light!"

Pablo switched off the light, and the two stood stiffly, side by side. Maria put her hands on the books to keep them from falling again.

"Take care of the sail . . . I'll handle the wheel!" It was Red's voice. He said something else, but his words were drowned out by the wailing wind.

Suddenly the books tumbled to the floor, and the children were thrown across the room. They landed in a heap on the bunk under the porthole.

"You all right?" gasped Maria.

"All right," said Pablo.

Maria got onto her knees and drew the curtain aside. The wind had blown the clouds from the sky, and the moonlight flooded the deck.

Ronnie and his father were standing looking up at the mainsail. Pablo pulled the curtain a few more inches to get a better view.

"Drop that mainsail!" Jim shouted above the wind. He nudged Ronnie. "Main halyard is jammed! Go up the mast."

"Me?" said Ronnie.

"You," said Jim. "Up the mast!"

Ronnie leaned back into the wind, his chin tilting higher and higher as he gazed up at the towering mainmast.

Jim stared at his son curiously. "What're you waiting for?"

Ronnie stood rooted to the deck. He seemed unable to move. A gust of wind whipped his jacket open as he stood there, his hands hanging at his sides.

At the helm, Red looked over his shoulder. "Jim, get going!"

"Go on, Ronnie," said Jim. "That's an order!"

Ronnie looked in Red's direction, still not moving.

The man caught the boy's desperate look. He turned to Jim. "That's a man's job!" shouted Red.

"Right!" said Jim. He eyed his son sternly. "He's going!"

"Jim!" said Red, "He can't . . ."

"Let him try!" interrupted Jim. He waited for a moment for the wind to die down. Then he said evenly, "Go on. Nothing to be afraid of."

"I'm not afraid," the boy said. He clenched his fists and started for the mast.

Maria held her own fists clenched as she watched Ronnie make his way to the mast. Just as he reached out to grab hold of it, the ship heeled to take a heavy swell, and the boy stumbled.

"Steady . . . okay . . . *now*!" said Jim as Ronnie grasped the mast with both hands.

"He can do it!" Jim said to Red.

Maria heard the man's words but noticed a worried look on his face.

Pablo whistled through his teeth, and Maria could feel her fingernails digging into her palms as Ronnie began to inch his way up the mast.

Up, up, he went as the ship pitched and plunged on the rough, swollen sea, and the wind screamed wildly around him.

Ronnie passed the main boom and climbed to the spreaders. He stopped and looked down. The ship bucked and rocked like a wild horse. The boy wrapped his arms and legs tightly around the spreaders and clung as if he were pasted there.

"Move!" yelled Jim. "Don't stop!"

But the boy held fast, locked in his place.

"Don't look down! You're all right!" hollered Red. "Just don't look down!"

"Keep going!" shouted Jim.

Maria could feel the perspiration on her upper lip in spite of the chill wind. She grabbed Pablo's arm as the ship dove into the crevice of a great wave.

A sudden flap of the sail unlocked Ronnie's grip, and he hung suspended, holding on to the spreaders with one hand while his body dangled over the deck like a fish on the end of a line.

Maria sucked in her breath. The ship crested the wave and threw Ronnie back into the mast. He wrapped himself around it. "Come down," Maria whispered urgently under her breath. "Slide down, down."

"Ronnie!" Jim yelled. "You can make it!"

34

"You can make it, rich kid," whispered Pablo tensely.

Ronnie looked up at the tip of the mast. He reached a hand over his head. He looked down. Then, slowly, clumsily, he began to shinny downward.

Not until Ronnie's feet hit the deck did anyone speak. He hung his head as he stood weaving unsteadily before his father.

Jim pushed the boy aside. "Okay, I'll do it," he said.

Ronnie slunk out of sight as Jim started up the mast.

Red watched over his shoulder. "Doesn't take any guts to do what you're not afraid of," he said into the wind.

6

Maria sat back down on the bunk and pulled Pablo down beside her. "Soon as it's quiet again, we'll get back to Little David," she said. "Then in the morning, before anyone is up, we'll get off the ship."

"Where will we be?"

"Ensenada, first port of call," said Maria. She raised the mattress of the bunk. There was a storage chest beneath it. She lifted the lid. "Get in," she said.

Pablo stepped into the chest and scrunched down. "Where you gonna be?"

She pointed. "In that locker."

"Okay," said Pablo.

Maria went to the standing locker and brought back a man's jacket. "Here, cover yourself with this," she said. "And remember, don't fall asleep."

"I won't," said Pablo. He lay down in the chest

under the bunk, and Maria closed the lid and slid the mattress back on.

In the locker, Maria lay on the floor snuggled in a fleece-lined coat. As her body warmed, her eyelids began to droop and she was afraid she might fall asleep. She sat up and opened her eyes wide. She mustn't fall asleep—she mustn't!

Everything depended on staying awake until all the others were asleep. Then she and Pablo would get back to Little David and Noches and Bandido in the storage locker. And as soon as the ship docked, they'd find a way to sneak off.

The fury of the wind had died down, but Maria could hear the crisp sound of water rushing under the keel, and she swayed to the motion of the boat as it tossed and pitched uncertainly. And, like the boat itself, Maria's thoughts tossed and pitched uncertainly in her mind. Supposing something went wrong? What if Bandido began to bark or Noches started to cackle? Supposing Little David woke up and began to cry? Supposing they got caught!

She remembered one of the stories Ol' Cappy had told. It was about the days of the pirates, and how enemies hiding on board were forced to walk the plank. Maria pictured herself slowly walking the plank, and her heart began to pound as she saw herself putting one foot before the other, making ready to meet her Maker in a cold, green, watery grave.

She shook her head. That was silly! People didn't go around walking planks these days. These days, people would simply be turned over to the *authorities*. The *authorities!* Maria's heart pounded harder, and she could hear the throbbing loudly inside her ears.

Then she took a deep breath. She would think good thoughts. So far, nobody had been caught. It was wrong to think bad thoughts. It would be all right. They would be all right. "Please, God," thought Maria anxiously, "let it be all right."

For a long time, she sat huddled in the locker, desperately trying to stay awake. Gradually, the sea became calmer. After a while, all that could be heard was the regular slap-slapping of water against the boat. Maria's arm had fallen asleep and she rubbed it. She kept at it a long time—as much to keep awake as to relieve the pins and needles.

There was the sound of footsteps coming down the companionway. A crack of light appeared under the locker door.

Maria heard the tinkle of glass. "Brandy," said Jim. "Warm you up." His voice sounded tired.

"Thanks," Red said.

"To a good night's sleep. We can both use it."

"Cheers," said Red dryly.

There was a pause while the men downed their drinks, then:

"I'm going to hit the sack. Good night," said Jim.

"Could we sit for a minute? I want to talk to you," Red said.

"Hold it 'til morning. I'm bushed."

"Won't take long," Red insisted.

"I know what you're going to say. All right. Say it." Jim's voice sounded angry.

"I thought I was skipper of this ship."

"Well?"

"I ordered *you* up the mast, not Ronnie."

"I'm his father."

"And I'm the skipper. I give the orders."

Jim's voice rose. "Why don't you lay it on the line? We're not talking about who gives orders, we're talking about Ronnie."

"All right, we're talking about Ronnie. The three of us are going to be living in close quarters a long time, so let's get things straight right now. I give the orders . . ." Then Red added quietly, "I can teach him a lot if you let me."

"Can you teach him courage?"

"He's just a scared, lonely, little boy."

"Before this summer's over, I'll make a man of him," said Jim.

"A real man doesn't have to prove it," said Red. "To himself . . . or anyone else. He's not afraid to be gentle . . . he can afford to be tender."

Jim snorted. "He got plenty of tenderness from his mother. And from his grandmother. Look where it got him. His mother took off after the divorce. Left him like a weak kitten behind her. His gentle grandmother can't keep him in school. What he needs is discipline."

There was silence. Then Red said, "Jim, I've been with you for a lot of years, and never interfered with your personal life. How you raise your son ashore is none of my business." He paused and then went on. "But you endangered the ship. And on this ship, my word is law . . . for you and for Ronnie. If there's any question about that, I'll sign off at Ensenada in the morning. Think it over."

The footsteps and the movement of the boat told Maria that Red had gone above, but the light remained on, and she knew Jim was still in the chart room.

A frightened, trapped feeling came over Maria. Maybe it would be best to give themselves up. But she was scared of Jim. He didn't seem beautiful to her anymore. He seemed stern and cold. Surely he'd turn them in to the *authorities*.

How did she get into this mess anyway? Why was she sitting in some U.S. man's ship alone and afraid? Why didn't Jim go up to sleep so she and Pablo could join Little David? How long would he sit there?

Maria thought of Aunt Carmen, and a lonely feeling, like a wet sheet, settled over her. She blinked her eyes and the tears began to slide down her face. She thought of the songs Aunt Carmen used to sing. She thought of the time that she had the measles and still wanted to go out and play. Aunt Carmen had made up a lullaby especially for her:

> Little bird, be still,
> Little bird, you will,
> Soon be winging away . . .
> Little bird, don't cry,
> Little bird, you'll fly,
> Tomorrow's another day . . .
> Little bird . . .

The crack of light under the door went out, and Maria could hear Jim making his way up the companionway. Soon she could go get Pablo.

Maria sighed. Thinking of Aunt Carmen made her feel better. She leaned her head against the locker wall and closed her eyes. She could almost hear Aunt Carmen singing:

> Little bird, you're young,
> You will fly among,
> Eagles soaring on high . . .
> You will grow up strong,
> Then he'll come along,
> And now away you will fly . . .
> Little bird . . . little bird . . . little . . .

The words of the song and the lovely melody spun around and around in Maria's head. "Little bird . . . little bird . . ." Inside her head she saw blue, green, purple—deep, dark purple. And the tune became a live thing, and the words sang themselves—"little bird . . . little bird winging away . . ." And blackness poured over the purple and the words and the melody. And the melody melted blackly, blacker, blackest—faded softly, soft, still . . . dreamy . . .

And Maria fell into a deep, sound sleep.

The cramp in her leg had awakened her, and Maria got up with a start. It took a moment to remember where she was. She felt a strong, rocking motion—the sea was still rough. The light coming from under the locker door was milky pale. Maria wondered about the others. Was Pablo still asleep? And Little David and the animals, how were they? She put her hand to the door, then drew it back quickly when she heard a voice.

"Let's talk, Ronnie," said Jim.

"Nothing to talk about," answered Ronnie.

"About last night," said Jim.

Maria had no choice but to listen.

"Forget it," Ronnie said.

"Since we're stuck with each other, let's make the best of it."

Ronnie didn't answer.

Jim went on. "Why don't we shake?"

Ronnie was silent.

"It's going to be a long voyage."

Still no answer from Ronnie.

"Okay, if that's the way you want it," said Jim. There was a long pause while Jim flipped the pages of a book. "I promised your grandmother I'd tutor you."

"I don't want to be tutored."

"We'll be in Ensenada soon. Today's lesson is Spanish," said Jim with a sigh. "All right, repeat after me. '¿*Cómo está?*' "

"I don't feel good," Ronnie said.

"You feel fine," said Jim irritated. "Now, repeat after me. '¿*Cómo está?*' "

Again, Ronnie fell silent.

" '¿*Cómo está?*' " said Jim. "That means, 'How are you?' Say it. '¿*Cómo está?*' "

Maria wished Ronnie would say it before his father exploded. Too late.

42

"Look, all you have to do is say it. '*¿Cómo está?!* *¿Cómo está?!*' "Come on," Jim yelled. "*¿Cómo está?!*"

"*Muy bien, gracias, señor!*" came Pablo's voice from deep inside the bunk space.

"What did you say?" said Jim.

"I didn't say anything," said Ronnie, looking around.

" '*¿Cómo está?*' " Jim repeated uncertainly.

"*Muy bien, muy bien, gracias, señor!*" Pablo's voice piped loudly.

Maria clapped her hand to her forehead.

Pablo was caught!

7

Maria unlatched the locker door and opened it a crack to look out.

Pablo stood, swaying like a jack-in-the-box, inside the bunk space. Maria had never seen him look so pale—almost yellow.

"What's going on?" Jim exclaimed. "Who are you?"

Pablo forced a grin. "Pablo Carlos Smith de Salvidar, *señor*," he said brightly.

"What?" said Jim.

"Pablo Carlos Smith de . . ."

"I heard you!" Jim said shortly. "What're you doing here?"

"Going on a voyage," piped Pablo. "I heard you say so. On a voyage around the world."

"You must be crazy!" said Jim.

"No, *señor*. We're going to find my Papa. My Papa

is a U.S. sailor. He will be glad we found him. He will thank you and . . ."

Jim turned to Ronnie. "You know anything about this? He a friend of yours?"

"I never saw him before," said Ronnie.

"Sure you did, rich kid," Pablo said.

"No, I didn't . . . wait . . . yes, I did," said Ronnie.

"I thought so!" said Jim. "You better do some fast talking!"

"Some weirdo I saw on the pier. He's no friend of mine."

Jim looked closely first at Ronnie, then at Pablo.

"It's true," said Pablo. "I am no friend of his."

"What's all the ruckus about?" said Red as he came up behind Jim. Then he saw Pablo. "Well, I'll be . . . it's one of the box kids!"

"Good morning, *Señor* Red Hannigan," said Pablo.

"Is everybody crazy? Who is he?" Jim shouted.

"Pablo Carlos Smith de Salvidar," repeated Pablo patiently.

"One of those kids who lives in the box," said Red.

Jim lifted Pablo out of the bunk. The boy swayed unsteadily. He rolled his eyes, and his face grew a pasty green. Jim looked down at him. "Okay," said Jim, "talk!"

Pablo looked up at Jim. Then his head fell forward as though a spring had broken loose in his neck.

"Uh, oh . . ." said Red. The big man scooped Pablo up into his arms and rushed up the companionway with him.

Maria forgot herself and leaned forward too eagerly. The door swung open, and she fell headlong on the floor at Jim's feet. She struggled to get up, but her feet were spaghetti-limp and she fell backward, landing hard on her bottom.

"Oh, no!" said Jim in astonishment. "There's two of them!"

Maria looked up, dizzily trying to focus her eyes on Jim. "That's strange," she thought. "There are two of him, too." She felt hot, then cold, and she began to tremble.

Jim helped her to her feet and put her in a chair. "All right, you talk," he said. "And try to make some sense!"

"The *authorities* . . . they dumped our house on a garbage truck, so we couldn't go back to shore," said Maria.

Bewildered, Jim stared at her. "Tell me who you are."

"Maria Josefina Smith de Saldivar."

"You're related to . . . what's his name?"

"Pablo Carlos Smith de . . ." Maria started to say.

"Yeah, I know. How'd you get on this ship . . . what're you doing here?"

Maria looked up at Jim. The swinging lamp behind him caught her eye. She stared at it, her head swimming.

"I saw her with that other one. The weirdo . . . on the pier," said Ronnie.

"You want to start at the beginning?" said Jim.

Maria nodded. She would like to explain. But she

46

couldn't seem to take her eyes off the swinging lamp, and she felt a strange, oily warmness churning in the pit of her stomach.

Red came down the companionway, carrying a drained Pablo. He put the boy on the bunk. "Just a little seasick. He'll be all right."

Pablo looked at Maria. He started to say something, then he groaned and lay down.

Red turned. "Another box kid!"

"What the devil's a box kid?" said Jim.

"One of those kids who live in a box," Red said.

Jim shook his head in despair, then turned back to Maria. "You were saying?"

Maria felt sick to her stomach and clapped her hands over her mouth.

"Out of the way!" said Red, as he pushed Jim aside.

Maria felt herself being lifted in Red's strong arms. In a moment, they were up the companionway and onto the deck. The fresh air hit her like a slap in the face. She took a deep gulp as Red put her down at the rail. Holding onto the rail with both hands, she let the sickness have its way.

Red's arm was holding her up. "It's all right," said Red. He wiped her mouth with his handkerchief. "When you're seasick, you only *feel* like you're going to die."

When the heaving was over, and she could stand again, Maria looked into Red's eyes. He smiled. The kindness was almost too much for her and she fell into his arms. And she cried and cried until there were no tears left.

Red carried Maria back down into the chart room, and put her on the bunk, foot to foot with Pablo.

Jim came up as if to question her further. "Not now," said Red. "Give her a chance. She's sick."

"Then maybe you can throw some light on the subject," said Jim. "What did you mean, *box kids*?"

"I've been watching them for weeks. A woman used to come get them at night . . . then, when . . ."

He was stopped by the loud screeching of a rooster crowing.

Dumbfounded, Jim, Ronnie, and Red stared at Noches as he floated from the top step of the companionway to the floor.

Noches spread his wings. *Cockle-doodle-doo!* he shrieked.

Before anyone could speak, Bandido appeared at the top of the companionway and slid down to the floor unceremoniously. Slipping and sliding over the chart room floor, the dog made his way to Pablo, leaped upon the boy, and began licking his face.

"I gotta go to the bathroom!" All eyes turned to the top of the companionway. Little David was standing on the top step.

Maria raised herself up on one elbow, and Pablo sat up. Little David came down the companionway backward. His feet seemed to be made of rubber bands as he stood there trying to keep his balance. Suddenly, he clutched at his stomach.

Red strode to his side and bolted with him up the companionway before the little boy could get sick all over the chart room.

Ronnie spoke in a strained voice. "Dad?"

Jim looked down at his son. The boy's face was drawn and his eyes were glassy.

"I think I'm sick," said Ronnie.

Jim grabbed Ronnie's arm and pulled him to the companionway. "Quick!" he said. "On deck!"

Maria sighed weakly as she watched them make for the deck.

8

All day long the four children lay stretched out on the deck. Jim applied cold compresses to foreheads, and administered seasickness remedies. He tripped over Bandido and Noches . . . and mumbled under his breath. Red spoon-fed the patients weak tea, gave them crackers, and chuckled good-humoredly at Jim's frustration.

By dinnertime, the kids were completely recovered and hungry for the good meal Red put before them. Worried as she was about what would happen next, even Maria couldn't resist the fine food, and especially the hot apple pie Red had baked for them.

Jim came into the galley from the deck. "Here it comes," thought Maria gloomily. "Now he's going to tell us that he's turning us over to the *authorities*."

"I've given this a lot of thought," announced Jim. "We're heading back to San Diego."

"Pie?" said Red to Jim.

"No, thanks," said Jim. "Their aunt will be looking for them," he added by way of explanation.

Ronnie put his fork across his plate. Little David, sitting next to Ronnie, put his fork across his plate and smiled up at the older boy.

"Nothing else to do," said Jim.

Nobody answered.

Then Red said, "Finish your milk, Ronnie."

Ronnie drained his glass. Little David drained his glass.

"What would you suggest I do?" said Jim.

"Have some pie," said Red.

Jim began to pace in the small galley. "This is ridiculous!"

"Once we're in Mexican waters, I won't have time to bake. Gonna do a lot of fishing," said Red, putting a piece of pie in a plate.

Jim picked up the plate then put it back down. "I'd have to be out of my mind . . ."

Red put the plate in Jim's hand. "Go ahead, it's good."

"You expect me to go around the world with a bunch of strange kids?"

Red nodded to the plate in Jim's hand. "Try it," he said.

Jim put the plate down. "No, thanks! I'm not traveling around with a flock of children . . . and livestock!"

Jim went on: "Long-lost fathers! Sick kids! Poultry!"

"And dogs," said Little David innocently.

"And dogs!" sputtered Jim. "There's no place on this ship for dogs . . . or children!"

Ronnie stiffened and folded his arms. Little David folded his arms.

"We'll head back to San Diego," said Jim. "And that's final!"

Maria caught Red's eye. "Do something," she thought. "Please."

"Look, Jim," Red said. "We're closer to Ensenada. Why not anchor there tonight? Decide about the children in the morning."

Jim stopped pacing. All eyes were on him as he answered. "Okay. Ensenada it is," he said.

"Good," said Red. "I plan to do some fishing in these waters tomorrow."

Then Jim added, "Okay, but I turn these kids over to the Mexican authorities first thing in the morning."

Maria and Pablo exchanged anxious glances. Their last hope was gone.

Little David moved closer to Ronnie and took his hand.

Ronnie pretended not to notice, but he didn't move his hand.

The children had been sent to their cabin early. Maria and Ronnie occupied lower bunks opposite each other. Pablo and Little David had the top bunks. Bandido and Noches were on the floor.

"It's strange," thought Maria. "Last night, I couldn't stay awake; tonight, I can't go to sleep." The others were awake, too. Maria could feel it even though nobody had spoken for half an hour.

Finally, Pablo broke the silence. "I'm not sleepy," he said.

"Me, too," said Little David.

"Wonder how old we'll be when we get out of jail," Pablo said.

Little David began to whimper.

"You talk too much," said Ronnie.

Again, there was silence, each of the kids thinking his own dark thoughts.

"Hey, rich kid," said Pablo.

Ronnie kept quiet.

"Hey, *muchacho rico*, why you always mad?"

"Hey, dumb kid," Ronnie mimicked, "why you always talk so much?"

"I wanna go home," said Little David.

"Go to sleep, all of you," said Maria.

"Weirdo . . ." Ronnie mumbled.

Maria sat up. "Pablo's right. You're always mad."

"What's it to you?" answered Ronnie.

"What makes you like that?" said Maria. "You got a grandmother, you got a ship, you got a father . . ."

"Sure, I got a father," Ronnie broke in. "And he's gonna dump me sure as he's gonna dump you."

Now, there was quiet again. Maria looked over at Ronnie. He was lying on his back, staring straight up. She couldn't help feeling sorry for him. She slipped out of her bunk and got down on her knees.

"Sweet Virgin, Mother of God," Maria prayed. "Forgive us. We didn't mean to make trouble. Please, God, don't give us to the *authorities*. We'll be good

54

from now on, I promise. I'll even make a spiritual bouquet like Father Ramires said: I'll say ten rosaries, I'll go to confession and communion ten times, I'll say the Litany to the Saints ten times, and offer all of this up to the Blessed Mother . . . ten times." Maria sighed. "Twenty times . . ." Then she said, "God bless Aunt Carmen and Pablo and Little David and Noches and Bandido." She stood up, then got back down on her knees. "And God bless Jim and Red and Ronnie. Amen."

"What's that all about?" asked Ronnie.

"I was praying," said Maria softly. "Praying for us, for you . . . and for both our fathers."

Back in her bunk, Maria turned on her side and looked at Ronnie. He had covered his head with the blanket and turned to face the wall.

For a long time, Maria lay wondering about the rich kid who was so miserable. He had everything Maria could think of to make a boy happy, and yet, he was like a stray dog, ready to snap and bark at everybody.

Maria watched Bandido jump to the foot of Ronnie's bunk. The boy, without uncovering his head, pushed him off with his foot. But Bandido soon leaped up again. The bed was more comfortable than the floor. Again, the boy pushed him off with his foot.

Maria reached out, lifted up Bandido, and put him on the foot of her own bunk. When she looked back over at Ronnie, Little David was standing beside him. He had climbed down and had reached out to touch Ronnie's shoulder. His head still covered, Ronnie pushed Little David's hand away. Maria smiled. Ronnie must think Little David was the dog. She watched curiously, waiting to see what would happen. Little David touched Ronnie again. This time Ronnie sat up and looked full in the small boy's face. Then he moved over, pulled Little David into his bunk, and covered him with his blanket.

It was late at night, and still Maria couldn't fall asleep. The boys were asleep. Bandido was asleep. Noches was asleep. "The whole world must be asleep except for me," thought Maria. "No. Aunt Carmen wouldn't be asleep. No matter where she is she'd be thinking of us. She'd be wondering where we are . . . what we're doing."

If she could only think hard enough, maybe Aunt Carmen would hear her thoughts. Maria squeezed her eyes shut tightly. If she had any wish in the whole world, it would be to be back with Aunt Carmen. Right now, right this minute, she wished they could be together again like they used to be. Someday they would find Papa, but, for the moment, all she could wish for was her beloved Aunt Carmen.

Maria sat up and looked around the tiny cabin. Could Aunt Carmen hear her wish? Perhaps if she were outdoors, her thoughts could fly more freely. She wrapped her blanket around her shoulders and stole quietly up to the deck.

The vast, empty sea was flooded with moonlight, and a fine, spanking breeze ruffled the water. A shoal of flying fish rose, then skimmed away to plunge back into the sea. Maria took a deep breath of the salty air and made her wish.

"Coffee?" she heard Red's voice across the deck.

Maria turned. Jim, standing watch at the helm, took the mug of steaming coffee that was held out to him and sipped.

Maria pulled her blanket close around her and leaned back into the shadows.

"I know what you're thinking," said Jim.

Red looked at the other man.

"The answer is, 'no,' " Jim said.

Red said nothing.

"Now, look, Red. I'm not going to keep those kids. I'm not going to float around the world on some crazy, mindless search."

"I'll take over the wheel," said Red. The two men changed places.

"You just can't pick up a stray bunch of kids and take off with them," said Jim.

"I've been watching them on the beach for weeks," answered Red. "I asked a few questions. The aunt's out of the picture . . . a couple of months, at least. There's nobody else. The little one's been abandoned. If we took them . . . just for a while, who'd be the wiser?"

"Got enough trouble with my own kid."

Red said nothing, his silence more potent than words.

"Besides, those others are none of my business."

"Guess not," grunted Red.

"See you in the morning," said Jim. "I'm going to hit the sack."

9

Maria crept back down and into her berth. They would go to jail and it was all her fault. She was the oldest. She shouldn't have listened to Pablo. She should have waited for a sign before they boarded the boat that terrible night.

She shuddered. She'd heard about *reformatórios*—jails for bad children. Once Pablo took a pair of sunglasses from a stall in Tijuana. The old lady who tended the stall had screamed at him. "You belong in the *reformatório!* With all the other rotten criminals!" Pablo had cried; he was only seven at the time.

"Where rats play on your belly while you sleep, and the mattress stinks!" the old woman had cackled.

It was only after Aunt Carmen had come and paid

for the sunglasses, and pleaded with the old lady to spare her poor, orphaned nephew, that the woman relented and grudgingly agreed not to turn Pablo over to the police.

"Mark my words," she had screeched after them, "mark my words, that thief will spend his days in a cage!"

And that was only for attempting to steal a pair of sunglasses. What happens to children who attempt to steal a whole ship? It was too awesome to think about.

After a long while Maria fell into a fitful sleep . . .

And it was almost too real to be a dream. She was in a tiny cage. The air was so bad, it almost choked her. There were four cells opposite her. In the first one sat Pablo dressed in rags. Little David was clutching the bars of the second cell. He was wearing huge, dark sunglasses, and crying, "I wanna go home!" Bandido was running frantically in circles in a cell of his own, and Noches, flapping his wings, was perched on a crossbar in his own cage.

Now, the two authorities Maria had seen on the beach came by. They each had a basket of moldy bread, and they began throwing hunks of it at the prisoners. Maria was pelted with the rocklike pieces of bread until she was covered with great red welts. "Stop!" she screamed. "We'll confess . . . we'll confess!"

"We'll confess!" hollered Pablo.

"Me, too!" cried Little David from behind the sunglasses.

Bandido clawed at the bars of the cage and barked wildly. Noches, clucking crazily, ruffled his feathers.

"We confess! We did it! We stole the ship!" cried Maria. "Don't hit us anymore!"

"Have pity!" yelled Pablo. "You're hurting me!"

"Me, too!" screamed Little David.

Suddenly, they were in the chart room of the *St. Agnes*. Ronnie, dressed as a judge, was sitting behind a desk. "I will now pronounce sentence," he said gravely.

"I wanna go home!" cried Little David.

"Why you always so mad, rich kid?" said Pablo.

"Shut up, weirdo," said Ronnie. "This is my father's ship."

Two rats skittered into the room from a tiny hole under the bunk. Horrified, Maria watched while dozens more crowded into the chart room. Ronnie vanished as the room filled with squealing rats.

"Up here!" cried Maria as she scampered up on the desk. She helped Little David and Pablo scramble up.

On the floor, the rats were nipping at Bandido. He yipped and barked as he tried to fight them off. It was no use. There were too many of them. Soon he was buried under hundreds of rats.

Noches rose above the squeaking animals and flew to the desk. There was a rat hanging onto his tail. Maria tried to kick it off with her foot, but it hung on. Noches let out an ear-shattering *Cockle-doodle-doo-ooo*!

60

Maria sat bolt upright, awakened by the sound. She looked around.

Cockle-doodle-doo! Noches cried from Little David's empty bunk above Ronnie's.

It was morning.

The children were almost dressed when there was a knock at the door. "Breakfast! Fifteen minutes!" called Red.

"I'm starving," said Pablo.

"Me, too," said Little David.

"Is food all you can think about?" said Ronnie sarcastically.

"You got something better to think about, rich kid?"

"Yeah, I've got a plan."

"What plan?" said Maria.

"A way to get you off this boat before you're turned over to the authorities."

Pablo sat down on Maria's bunk and looked closely at Ronnie. "You'd help us get away?" he said.

"That's what I said, weirdo."

"Why?" said Pablo suspiciously. "Since when do you want to help us?"

"I don't."

"Then what are you talking about?" said Maria.

"Just this. You want to get away from the authorities, I want to get away from my old man. You help me, I help you. Get it?"

"No," said Maria.

"I'll spell it out. I'm not waiting 'til my father dumps me. I'll dump him first. But I can't do it alone.

I know how we can all get away together. Then you go your way and I'll go mine."

"What's the plan?" said Pablo.

"First, we figure a way to get sent to our cabin early tonight. Then, when it's quiet, we lower the dinghy and take off."

"I don't know . . ." said Maria dubiously.

"Sounds easy," said Pablo.

"It is. It's a cinch."

"We'll be heard," said Maria.

"Not if we're quiet," answered Ronnie.

"How can we get sent to our cabin early?" asked Maria.

"I got that figured out. Something I worked out when I was in one of those dumb schools. It's foolproof."

"What do we have to do?" said Pablo.

"Before I tell you, are we all agreed?" asked Ronnie looking at Maria. "Have we got a deal?"

Maria nodded. "Agreed."

"Deal," said Pablo.

"Okay, then. Here's the plan. We throw a hunger strike."

"What?" said Pablo.

"A hunger strike, stupid. It always works. Grown-ups go nuts when kids don't eat. We'll get sent to our cabin sure as we're sitting here."

"You mean we don't eat supper?"

"I mean we don't eat anything . . . all day."

"All day!" exclaimed Pablo.

"You wanna get away from the authorities, don't you?" said Ronnie.

"Sure, but why not just skip supper?"

"That won't work. One meal won't matter. Believe me, I know. If we don't eat anything all day, they'll think we're dying by dark. Then we make our move."

The other three children looked at each other saying nothing.

"Well?" said Ronnie. "You wanna get off this tub or not?"

"What do you say?" said Pablo to Maria.

"Okay," said Maria.

"Little David?" said Pablo.

"Okay," said Little David.

"Wait a minute. Little David can't go without food all day," said Maria.

"I thought of that," answered Ronnie. He pulled a candy bar out of his pocket and handed it to the little boy. "Eat this," he said.

Little David smiled up at Ronnie, beaming with affection.

Embarrassed, Ronnie moved back. "All right, all right," he said gruffly. "You get another one at lunchtime."

"Hey, how many of those have you got?" asked Pablo.

"Only enough for Little David. You starve like the rest of us."

Pablo sighed. "This better work."

"It'll work," said Ronnie.

"How do you *know*?" asked Maria. "What happens if it doesn't work?"

"Just leave it to me," said Ronnie. "As long as we stick together, it'll work. Now, let's go *not* eat breakfast."

10

Crisp bacon surrounded the plates of steaming, scrambled eggs. Red brought a huge platter of hot biscuits and set it on the galley table. He poured Jim a cup of coffee. "Dig in," he said to the others, taking a seat at the table.

Jim and Red started to eat, but the children sat with their hands in their laps.

"Biscuits are great," said Jim. "Pass the jam."

Red passed the jam pot and put a biscuit on each of the children's plates. Little David started to take his biscuit. But Pablo kicked him under the table and he looked at the other kids, then put the biscuit down. Red glanced around the table, stopped eating, and put his fork down.

Jim was the only one eating. Soon he looked up. "What's the matter with all of you? Isn't anyone going to eat?" he said. He passed the jam to Maria. "Blue-berry . . . delicious."

"No, thank you," said Maria.

"Ronnie?" Jim said.

"I'm not hungry," said Ronnie.

"Me, too," said Little David.

"I suppose you're not hungry, either," Jim said to Red.

The older man shrugged.

"Well, I'm starving," said Jim as he attacked his bacon and eggs.

He ate as the others watched and, when he was through, he helped himself to more coffee.

"I've had enough of this foolishness. Ronnie, eat your breakfast!" said Jim. "You won't get me to change my mind this way."

Ronnie shook his head.

Exasperated, Jim turned to Red. "What in the devil do you expect of me? You know I can't take these kids with us!"

Red rose and began clearing the table.

"I couldn't get away with it, even if I wanted to . . . which I don't!"

"More coffee?" said Red.

"It wouldn't be legal!" said Jim.

Red poured the remainder of the coffee into Jim's cup and moved to the sink.

Little David's stomach growled.

"You think money can buy anything? Well, it can't!" said Jim. "My lawyers! Ha! You think they can legal-ize a crazy situation like this? Well, they can't."

66

Little David's eyes were on the biscuit plate as Red removed it from the table.

"Kidnapping! That's what it would be! Kidnapping!"

"Finished?" said Red.

"Child stealing!" Jim went on. "Rustling, if you consider the livestock these kids have!"

Maria licked her lips as she watched Red scrape her untouched eggs and bacon onto a larger platter.

"Kidnapping's a federal offense, you know that?" said Jim.

"I know," said Red.

"We could all land in the federal penitentiary!"

Red put the platter of leftovers on the sink and came back for the toast.

"Kids ought to be in school . . . given a chance," said Jim.

"I don't go to school," said Little David.

Jim ignored the boy. "We could create an international incident! Did you think of that when you accused me of being hardhearted?"

"I never accused you of . . ." Red began.

"That's what you're thinking, isn't it?"

"May I be excused?" said Ronnie.

Jim sighed. "Yes, you're excused. You're all excused. Go up on deck . . . all of you."

Lunch was almost a carbon copy of breakfast. Only the menu was different: salad, crisp fried fish and mashed potatoes, tiny green peas, and chocolate pudding with whipped cream. But the children politely and firmly refused to eat a bite. Little David was about to give in when the chocolate pudding came around, but Ronnie quickly slipped him a candy bar under the table.

At first Jim pretended not to notice the children's refusal of food. He ate heartily and with great relish. Then he angrily ordered them away from the table and turned on Red. "You haven't eaten a thing all day! What kind of example are you? Aiding and abetting those crazy kids in their crazy scheme!"

But Red only smiled. "Sympathy," he said. "For the strikers."

Supper was different. "All right, you kids," Jim announced firmly. "The strike is over. You'll eat if you have to sit here until morning!"

Alarmed, Maria flashed a look at Ronnie. But the boy sat smiling benignly.

"Pick up your spoons," said Jim.

The kids did as they were told.

"Now eat that soup!"

The kids put their spoons down.

Jim dipped his own spoon into Ronnie's bowl. "Open your mouth," he said, holding the spoon to the boy's mouth. Ronnie clamped his mouth shut and turned his face away.

Jim turned to Little David and held the spoon to his mouth.

"Eat!" he ordered.

Little David tightened his lips and his eyes rolled up. The hot soup in the bowl steamed up into his face. He suddenly hiccuped loudly.

"Open your mouth!" said Jim.

Little David opened his mouth.

"Now eat!" said Jim, putting the spoonful of soup into Little David's mouth.

At that instant, Little David was convulsed with a series of hiccups. He sucked the soup into his throat and began to cough and sputter. He raised his hands to cover his mouth and sent the spoon flying across the room. Gasping for breath, his face grew bright red and tears squeezed out of his eyes.

Red crossed quickly to his side and wacked him hard on the back. The boy wheezed, trying to catch his breath. "Water," said Red. Jim brought the boy a glass of water and put it to his mouth. Then Little David was shaken with another violent hiccup. His chin hit the top of the glass and dumped the water into Jim's lap.

Jim rose, the water running down his pant legs. "Out!" he yelled pointing to the doorway. "Out of my sight . . . all of you! Go to your cabin and get into bed! I've had about all I can stand for one day! Now march!"

Ronnie lifted the still-hiccuping Little David in his arms and carried the boy out. The other kids followed triumphantly.

The children were in luck. It was a black, windless night, and nobody was on watch. Once on deck, it was only a matter of getting the dinghy lowered swiftly and quietly into the water.

The dinghy was suspended on its side by ropes stretching from the davits, the metal arms on each end of the stern.

They kept their voices down.

"Maria, keep Little David and the animals back," whispered Ronnie. He turned to Pablo. "First, we loosen the ropes, then when I say 'go' we lower the dinghy."

"Right," said Pablo.

"Wait until I say 'go.' It has to be lowered evenly."

"I get it," Pablo said.

The boys unwound the ropes around the davits. "Go," said Ronnie as he let his rope slip slowly through the pulley.

The sudden weight of the dinghy pulled Pablo's rope through the pulley faster than he expected. And before he could stop it, the bow of the little boat landed upright in the water, bringing Ronnie's side slamming into the stern.

"Grab it!" said Ronnie. "Before it sinks!"

Pablo let go of the rope and reached over to steady the dinghy before it could slam into the stern again. He bent far over the rail clawing the air with both hands. Now, he felt the little boat brush his arm, and he made a wide grab for it. Reaching too far, he catapulted over the side, and with a great splash, hit the cold water below.

Instantly, Maria was at the stern, searching the water for a sign of Pablo. Then she saw his head bob to the surface. "Are you all right?" she cried.

"All right," Pablo sputtered.

"Maria . . . hold the rope . . . the dinghy's sinking!" said Ronnie.

Maria tried, but the rope slipped through her hands. "I can't hold it," she said.

"What's going on?" Red's voice called.

"They're not in their cabin . . . where're the kids?" came Jim's voice.

The water in the bow of the dinghy pulled the rope burning through Maria's palms. Letting go, she put her smarting hands to her mouth.

Now, all the weight was on Ronnie's side. He snatched the rope in front of the davit and hung on with all his strength. Then Maria watched in horror as Ronnie, still holding onto the rope, disappeared over the side. She heard a loud splash as Ronnie was dumped into the sea.

Suddenly Red was beside Maria, throwing a life ring to Pablo. "Hold onto this!" he shouted. Then Ronnie's head sprang up next to Pablo's. "Hang on . . . both of you!" Red yelled.

Now Jim appeared. "What is it? What's happening?"

"It's all right," said Red. "Get the other side of the dinghy before we lose her."

Working together, the men secured the dinghy and then towed the boys in.

Everyone was assembled in the chart room.

"You could have been drowned, seriously hurt. You

could have lost our lifeboat," said Jim angrily. "And I want to know who's responsible."

The kids stood before him looking down at the floor. Pablo wrapped Red's robe more tightly around himself and tried to keep his teeth from chattering. Ronnie, holding a towel draped over his shoulders like a huge cloak, sneezed loudly.

"Do you have anything to say, Ronnie?" asked Jim.

"No," said Ronnie.

"Pablo?"

"No."

"How about you, Maria?"

"No, *señor*," said Maria.

"Little David?"

Little David looked at Ronnie. The older boy shook his head. Little David shook his head.

"All right, then. Ronnie, as the eldest, I'm holding you fully responsible. Tomorrow, after we leave these kids with the authorities, we're heading for home . . . and school. Now go to bed . . . and stay there."

For a moment, Ronnie stared at his father, then he turned away and started to leave.

"Wait," said Maria. "*Señor*, it wasn't his fault. It was ours. He was just trying to help us."

"Ronnie?" said Jim.

Still the boy said nothing.

"Don't put him in one of those dumb schools, *señor*," said Maria. "He hates it there."

"Yeah," said Pablo. "He was only trying to help us get the dinghy in the water so we could get away from the *authorities*."

"How about it, Ronnie?" said Jim.

"He's lying. I was going to run away. *They* were helping *me*."

"Who's lying?" Pablo said.

"You are, weirdo," said Ronnie.

"So are you, rich kid," said Pablo.

Jim sighed. "One of you is lying, that's for sure."

"Maybe Little David can tell us," said Red. "Who's telling the truth, son?"

"They both are," said Little David brightly.

The men sat looking puzzled while, over the small boy's head, Pablo and Ronnie looked at each other and grinned.

II

The dinghy was in the water beside the *St. Agnes.* Jim, in the dinghy, helped Maria into the little boat. Pablo, holding Bandido in his arms, was lowered by Red. Jim put Pablo and Bandido in the seat next to Maria. Now Red, up in the *St. Agnes,* leaned over the rail and gave Jim the rooster. Jim handed it to Maria.

Red turned to Little David. The boy ran to Ronnie and hid behind him. "Come on, son," said Red. "Let's go."

"I won't!" cried Little David. "I don't wanna go!" He clung to Ronnie until the older boy picked him up. "Don't let them take me! Please, Ronnie! I don't wanna go to the *'formatório!'*"

"Let him stay. Please," Ronnie whispered to Red.

"Sorry, Ronnie," Red said. "He goes, too." As gently as he could, Red wrenched the sobbing Little David from Ronnie's arms and lowered him to Jim and the waiting dinghy.

Ronnie stood at the rail beside Red and watched bleakly as the dinghy took off.

Through the blur of tears, Maria couldn't tell for sure, but she thought she saw tears in the boy's eyes, too.

In town, Jim took the children to a low-slung stucco building with a red tile roof. Over the doorway were the words, *Administración Público.*

Maria wondered what Jim was telling the Mexican officials. She would have liked to tell *their* side of it. But they had to wait in a little anteroom under the watchful eye of a Mexican policeman while Jim consulted with the sergeant. The policeman wore a great bunch of dangling keys at his waist.

When Jim came back out into the anteroom, he wouldn't look the children straight in the eye, but he made some attempt to say good-bye. He told them to be good and to eat lunch when it was served. He told them not to be afraid; they'd be sent back to Tijuana to wait for their aunt. They'd be safe and cared for. "Sure, we'll be safe," thought Maria. "We'll be safe in the *reformatório.*"

Jim put his hand in his pocket and gave them each a dollar. "For ice cream," he said, "on the trip back to the bordertown." Then he strode quickly out of the building without looking back.

The policeman took the children and their animals

to a waiting room in the administration building, and told them to stay there. He closed the door behind him, and the kids could hear the key turn in the lock.

Maria and Little David sat on a hard, wooden bench with Noches while Pablo and Bandido walked around the room. The boy stopped at the lone barred window, which faced the back alley. He pulled a chair up to the window. "Maybe the bars are loose," Pablo said.

Maria sighed and shook her head. "They don't look loose."

Pablo shook the bars. "You're right," he said.

"I gotta go to the bathroom," said Little David.

Pablo's eyes lit up. "He's gotta go to the bathroom," he said jumping off the chair.

Maria looked at Pablo. "You think . . . ?" said Maria.

"We can try," said Pablo. He went to the door and began banging on it. "Hey, *señor!*" he shouted. "I gotta go to the bathroom!"

"Me, too!" yelled Little David. "I gotta go to the bathroom!"

"Come on," said Pablo to Maria. "Don't you gotta go to the bathroom?"

The three children banged on the door and shouted. "Open up! Hey, *señor!* Open the door! We gotta go!"

Bandido added to the din by barking furiously, and Noches cluck-clucked loudly.

Soon the children heard footsteps. "Remember," said Pablo. "When the door opens, run. We meet in back of the building. Okay?"

"Okay," said Maria.

"Everybody goes in a different direction. Got it?"

"Got it," Maria said.

"Me, too," said Little David.

A key turned in the lock. When the door opened the policeman was rushed by two boys, a girl, a dog, and a rooster—all yelling at the top of their lungs. "Run!" shouted Pablo.

"Stop!" cried the policeman. He reached out and caught Pablo.

"Run! Go! Run!" yelled Pablo as he squirmed out of the policeman's grasp.

Pablo raced down a long hall and ran headlong into an attendant carrying a lunch tray. Pablo's feet shot out from under him and the tray clattered to the floor. Covered with soup, refried beans, and tortillas, he was captured.

Maria ran the other way. She went through an inner door. Then without looking in either direction, she ran as fast as she could go. She stopped abruptly and found herself standing in front of a judge's bench in an open courtroom. The spectators began to laugh uproariously as the judge banged his gavel. "Take this child away!" he sputtered. "This is an outrage! Take the girl away!" Maria was captured.

Bandido made it as far as the main doorway. Then he was stopped, scooped up, and captured.

Noches was found perched on the circling ceiling fan in the anteroom very dizzy. He was captured.

It took a long time for the officials to find Little

David. But he was finally captured, too—in the bath-room.

Maria and Little David sat on the wooden bench in the waiting room while Pablo paced the room. Again, he stopped at the window.

"Hey, Maria," Pablo whispered. "Look!"

"It's no use," said Maria. "We can't move those bars."

"Come here, both of you!"

Little David got up on the chair, and Maria stood on tiptoe to peer out of the window.

Framed by the window and grinning widely, Ronnie was motioning to them excitedly.

"It's Ronnie!" said Little David, nearly falling off the chair with joy.

"Quiet, or we'll be heard," said Pablo. He lifted Little David off the chair. Then he mouthed to Ronnie, "We'll meet you. Stay there."

"How you gonna meet him?" asked Maria. "How we gonna get out of here?"

Pablo smiled and pulled a large key from out of his T-shirt. He dangled it in front of Maria, then held it up for Ronnie to see. "When that policeman grabbed me, I grabbed this," said Pablo proudly.

Ronnie clasped his hands together over his head and made the "win" sign.

"Now, listen," said Pablo. "We'll wait 'til it's quiet. Then we'll use the key. And this time, we stick to-gether. Okay?"

"Okay," said Maria.

"Okay," said Little David.

Pablo listened at the door. He turned the key and opened the door a crack. Then he shut it quickly. "Back to the bench," he said.

By the time the children were seated on the bench, they could hear footsteps coming closer. The footsteps stopped at the door, hesitated, then went on. Soon they could be heard no more.

Again, Pablo opened the door and cautiously peeked out. He waved the others to follow him. They walked single file down the hall. First, Pablo, then Bandido. Little David went next; then Maria holding Noches. Pablo turned a corner, then stepped back. "Two of them . . . coming this way!"

Behind them, they suddenly heard footsteps again. "We're caught!" whispered Maria.

"In there!" Little David said. He ran down the hall and opened a door marked, *Caballeros,* where he had been captured earlier. They all dashed into the men's room, and they saw a small, open window.

Pablo boosted Maria up. "Ronnie!" called Maria to Ronnie, standing a little way down the alley. "Help me!"

Ronnie caught the girl as she jumped to the ground. Then Maria and Ronnie helped Little David out. Bandido leaped off the sill himself, and Noches was next. Finally, Pablo squirmed out of the little window, and they were all outside.

"Come on," said Ronnie. "Let's get away from here!"

12

They followed Ronnie down the alley and into a side street. Then they ran for all they were worth, up one narrow street and down the next until Little David begged them to stop.

At the edge of the *zocolo*, the town square, was a clump of oleanders. They paused to rest. The public square was lined with vendors exhibiting their wares to the native shoppers and tourists milling around. Some of the stalls sold souvenirs, some silver jewelry, some candles, some pottery, and some good things to eat. The sweet smell of steaming corn and fresh-baked *tortillas* filled the air.

"How did you get away?" asked Pablo.

Ronnie laughed. "Red wanted to do a little fishing before they headed for home, so they left the dinghy in the water. I'm supposed to be in my cabin. They won't look for me until suppertime . . . I hope."

"Then we'd better move. But where?" said Pablo. "Where do we go from here?"

"Back to San Diego," said Maria. "Find another box to live in. Wait for Aunt Carmen, like before."

"What about you, Ronnie?" said Pablo. "Where are you headed?"

"I'm coming with you," Ronnie said.

"But your father . . ." said Maria.

"I'm coming with you."

"Good," said Pablo.

"Good," parroted Little David, snuggling closer to Ronnie.

"San Diego's a long way from here," said Maria.

"If we use public transportation, we'll be caught," said Ronnie. "My father will see to that."

"Maybe we can go by boat," said Pablo. "Hide out on another ship."

"How will we know where another ship is going?" said Maria.

The children fell silent. Then Ronnie said, "We'll have to walk. We can walk at night and sleep in the daytime. But we'll need some money." He emptied his pockets. All he had were coins. "Any of you got any money?" he asked.

"Your father gave us each a dollar," said Pablo. He took the dollar out of his pocket and gave it to Ronnie.

Maria gave her dollar to Ronnie, too. She turned to Little David. "We're putting all the money together. Give Ronnie your dollar."

"Here, Ronnie," said Little David. "You can have it."

Ronnie counted up the money: three dollars and seventy-eight cents.

"That's not much," said Maria shaking her head. "We'll need some things."

"What things?" asked Ronnie.

"Shoes—*huaraches*—we can't walk all the way to San Diego barefooted. And food, at least for tonight."

Pablo touched his driver's cap. "And three sombreros, to shade you from the sun."

"Okay, let's get the stuff and leave town before my father misses me, and the *authorities* miss you," said Ronnie.

At the word, *authorities*, they were on their way. They stopped at a souvenir shop, which had a large outdoor display of baskets of pottery, straw hats, rugs, candlesticks, and souvenir trinkets in front. Pablo picked up a leather key chain . . . souvenir of Ensenada. Pretending interest in the key chain, he said to Ronnie, "You go in. Buy the hats. We'll wait here and look out for the *authorities*."

They watched Ronnie go into the store. Then Maria saw the statues. She followed Ronnie in and stopped at a shelf of clay Madonnas. She put Noches under one arm and took a Madonna off the shelf. It was beautiful. Even prettier than the Madonna she had in San Diego.

Ronnie spoke to the storekeeper. "How much for the straw hats?" he said, pointing to a large hat on a shelf behind the man.

"Ten *pesos, señor*," said the storekeeper. "It's a fine *sombrero*. The best."

84

Ronnie looked at Maria questioningly. Maria shook her head. Then she put the Madonna carefully back on the shelf.

"I'll give you five *pesos*," said Ronnie.

"Eight *pesons, señor*," said the storekeeper.

Ronnie glanced at Maria. With one finger, she was stroking the Madonna on the shelf. She shook her head.

"Six *pesos*," said Ronnie to the storekeeper.

"Seven," said the storekeeper.

Maria nodded.

"Seven," agreed Ronnie. "I'll take three." He counted out the money and handed it to the storekeeper. Then he said, "How much for the Madonna?"

Maria looked up sharply.

"Ah, *señor*, that Madonna, she is the most beautiful. She is not cheap."

"I'll give you one dollar . . . American," said Ronnie.

Maria shook her head furiously.

"It is yours!" said the storekeeper jubilantly.

Ronnie put the Madonna into Maria's trembling hands. She felt a surge of joy but couldn't bring herself to speak. "She will bring us safely home," thought Maria as she clutched the little statue. "She will protect us from the *authorities*." She tucked the Madonna into her sweater pocket.

Once out of the store, Pablo took charge. "Follow me," he said to Ronnie ". . . but not too close. Maria, you and Little David walk behind us."

Ronnie nested all three *sombreros* together and put

them on his head. Then he and Pablo sauntered slowly past one stall after another. Pablo stopped at a corn cart. A huge tub of corn in boiling water sat on one end of the cart. Heaps of reddish, fresh corn on the cob were in a basket beside it. On the other side of the cart, ears of hot corn wrapped in paper were ready to be sold. "Buy one," whispered Pablo to Ronnie out of the side of his mouth.

Ronnie made the transaction. Then, while the vendor turned to make change, Pablo expertly snatched some of the paper-wrapped ears, and the vendor turned back just in time to see Pablo making off with his wares. Pablo ducked into the crowd, Ronnie right behind him. Maria took Little David's hand and raced after them.

"My corn!" shouted the vendor. "Stop!"

"Run!" yelled Pablo.

"Stop them!" roared the vendor. "Thieves! Stop!"

Maria and Little David caught up with Pablo and Ronnie. "Follow me!" Pablo said. He turned into a narrow alleyway, and the others raced behind him.

Maria looked over her shoulder. She could see the vendor turn into the alley. "He's coming!" she shouted, pulling Little David along.

Now Pablo plunged into the main street. There were throngs of tourists and shoppers inspecting the wares lining the avenue. He weaved his way down the street, Ronnie and Bandido at his heels.

"You're going too fast!" panted Little David. He suddenly halted, and Maria jerked his hand. The boy fell headlong into a huge basket of ripe tomatoes in front of a vegetable stall.

Maria set him back on his feet. "Come on!" she yelled as she pulled him after her.

For a moment Maria lost sight of Pablo and Ronnie. Then she saw them running toward a candy stand. She glanced back. Now the tomato man was following the first vendor. "Catch them!" he hollered. "Stop them!"

"Thieves!" shouted the corn man. "Get them!"

The candy vendor grabbed Pablo. Bandido nipped and danced at the man's ankles while the boy wrested himself loose and took off again. Ronnie, intent on rushing to Pablo's aid, ran smack into the candy cart, and his *sombreros* fell over his face. The man grabbed his shoulders. Ronnie's arms flailed in every direction. His sleeve caught on the handle of the cart, overturning it and spilling all of its contents on the ground. The man threw his hands up in dismay, and Ronnie darted away.

The next time Maria looked back she saw lollipops strewn all about, and the candy man, on his hands and knees, trying to retrieve the Mexican jumping beans that were hopping around on the ground. His peppery language followed them down the street.

A photographer's donkey cart blocked the exit at the end of the street. Pablo tried to get around it, but he couldn't. He crawled over the cart to get to the other side. "Come on!" he shouted to Ronnie. The donkey brayed as Ronnie climbed over the cart to join Pablo.

At this point, Noches flew out of Maria's arms and landed on the donkey's back. Maria pushed Little David over the cart as the startled donkey tried to buck the rooster off his back. He reared up on his hind legs, and Noches slid back down into Maria's arms as she clambered over the cart.

"*Jo! Burro, jo!*" yelled the photographer, trying to calm the animal. But the donkey, mad with fright, continued to paw the air, and knocked his hapless master to the ground on his seat—hard.

When Maria looked again, the corn man was trying to scramble over the cart. This time, it was too much for the poor donkey. Braying wildly, he turned and began to trot down the street after the kids, his master running behind him.

"I'm tired!" yelled Little David. "I can't run anymore!"

Pablo turned another corner and ran into the open door of a small church. The others, close behind, followed.

Pablo dipped his fingers into the bowl of holy water and made the sign of the cross. "In the name of the Father, the Son, and the Holy Spirit," he panted. He took Little David's hand and walked down the aisle of the empty church.

Maria dipped her fingers into the bowl of holy water and made the sign of the cross. Ronnie hesitated. "Go on," whispered Maria.

Ronnie put his fingers into the water and crossed himself. "In the name of the Father, the Son, and the Holy Spirit," Maria said for both of them.

88

Ronnie and Maria found places beside Pablo and Little David, and the four of them kneeled. At last, they could catch their breath. At once, Maria felt a kind of calm come over her. She closed her eyes. "We're in big trouble again, God," Maria prayed. "The *authorities* are after us, Ronnie's father is after us, the storekeepers are after us . . . oh, God, please help us."

They heard a loud commotion outside the church. They turned. The first vendor was striding angrily into the church.

The children, led by Maria, hurried down the church aisle. Maria knelt at the altar, then quickly turned toward the door at the side of the church.

Ronnie, right behind her, touched one knee to the floor and followed her. Passing the altar, Pablo brushed his knee to the floor and kept going. Little David, at Pablo's heels, managed only to bend his knees in a kind of curtsey before running out after the other kids.

In the courtyard, a flock of chickens and black roosters set up a clatter as the children raced toward the adobe wall. Noches flew out of Maria's arms and joined the flock.

"Catch him . . . catch Noches . . . he's loose!" cried Maria.

The children scampered after the bird, but it became impossible to tell which were the church roosters and which was Noches. Birds, children, and feathers flew all over the church courtyard.

A group of nuns filed into the courtyard. "What's

the meaning of all this?" said one of the sisters.

"Chicken thieves!" screamed another. *"Bandidos!"*

"Get them!" cried a third.

The children made it to the wall. When they paused, they looked at each other in amazement. Each one of them had a black rooster tucked under his arm!

"Over the wall!" cried Maria, holding tightly onto what she hoped was Noches. "Take the roosters!"

"Through the gate!" directed one of the nuns while the kids clambered over the wall. The sisters ran toward the gate, hoping to catch the children on the other side. But as they turned, they ran headlong into the storekeeper and vendors who were storming into the courtyard.

"Jesus, Mary, and Joseph!" cried one of the nuns as she picked herself up off the ground.

"Call the police!" shouted a storekeeper.

"Lord have mercy on us!" said a nun.

"Where are the thieves?" yelled the vendor of tomatoes.

Cockle-doodle-doo! screeched and indignant black rooster.

"Mother of God!" said another nun.

Cluck, cluck . . . caw, caw, buck, buck . . . buck cackled the chickens.

"There they go!" shouted the first vendor as he noticed Little David's legs go over the wall.

"After them!" cried the tomato man.

The kids ran down a little side street lined with small houses. Several dogs, cats, and small children took chase after them.

At the end of the street was an intersection. Suddenly, Pablo stopped dead. Little David stopped cold, behind him. Maria and Ronnie also came to a sudden stop.

Coming toward them were Jim and Red.

"There they are!" cried Jim breaking into a run.

Two policemen appeared from the left of the intersection. "That's them!" one of them yelled as they hurried forward.

The candy vendor, pushing his cart ahead of him, barreled into the intersection from the right. "Those are the ones!" he shouted pointing at the children.

Maria looked back. The nuns and storekeepers, joined by neighbors from the street, were closing in on them from the rear.

They were surrounded!

13

Back in the administration building, the whole crowd was brought before the judge. Everybody spoke at once.

"Who pays for the corn?" shouted the first vendor.

"A whole bushel of tomatoes . . . nothing but sauce now!" yelled the tomato man.

"To spite me? Is that why you ran off like that?" said Jim to Ronnie.

"My donkey . . . he's gone mad!" said the photographer.

"Chicken thieves!" hollered one of the nuns.

"Delinquents!" hollered another.

"Unlawful flight!" said one of the policemen.

"Resisting arrest!" said the other.

"God help me!" said the photographer. "My donkey will be good for nothing!"

"I wanna go home!" cried Little David.

"*Siléncio!*" shouted the judge above the din. He

rapped his gavel sharply. "Quiet! *Siléncio!*" He shook his head wearily. "First," he said, "let the children step forward."

There was a sudden silence as the kids moved up to the bench, each of them holding a black rooster under his arm.

"Put the poultry on the table," the judge intoned. "Exhibit A."

One by one, the children put a rooster on the table. "Which one is Noches?" wondered Maria as a sergeant tagged the squirming, clucking birds. "Or is Noches still back in the church courtyard among all those strange chickens?"

The judge looked closely at each one of the children. Little David's face was streaked with dirt, tomatoes, and tears. He was standing forlornly in a puddle of tomato juice. Ronnie's T-shirt was torn from the shoulder to the hem. He was bleeding at the elbow. Maria, wide-eyed and trembling, was clutching her clay Madonna and mouthing a silent prayer.

The judge's eyes held on Pablo. The boy's entire body looked bumpy and misshapen. Bandido lay across his bare feet. The judge nodded to one of the policemen. "Search him," he said.

From Pablo's back pocket, the policeman took a handful of Mexican jumping beans; there were two ears of corn under his T-shirt; a number of pointed lollipops were found in his left side-pocket; in his right pocket, a glob of squashed tomatoes. "Exhibits B, C, D, and E," said the judge, trying to hide a smile.

The policeman tried to wrest the clay Madonna

from Maria. "No!" shouted Ronnie. "That's bought and paid for . . . *legal!*"

"Is that right?" asked the judge of Maria.

"Yes, it's paid for. One dollar, American!" said Maria.

The judge sighed. "Let the girl have her statue," he said.

Cockle doodle-doo! cried one of the birds as he took wing and circled the room.

Again, everyone spoke at once while the two policemen chased the bird, upsetting chairs and benches. The rooster finally came to land on Maria's shoulder.

"Noches!" exclaimed Maria as she took the bird in her arms. "It's Noches!"

The judge rapped his gavel. "Quiet!" he commanded. The hubbub died down, and the judge doled out his verdicts. The nuns were given the remaining three birds and told to go back to the church and pray for the misguided children. Jim was to pay for any and all damage inflicted on the people and property of the town, and a whopping fine on top of that. He was also to gain custody of his own child. The other culprits were to be put back in the detaining room, this time with a guard stationed outside the door.

The judge wiped his brow with a handkerchief. "This case is dismissed," he said. "Court adjourned for *siesta*."

While Jim and Red paid the damages, Maria put Noches in Ronnie's arms. "Take good care of him," she said. "He won't like it in the *reformatório*." Ronnie nodded gravely.

Then Pablo took Bandido to Ronnie. "We'll come back for him someday." He put out his hand, and the two boys shook solemnly.

Ronnie watched sadly, swallowing a lump in his throat as the policeman led the children away.

It was late afternoon. *Siesta* time was nearly over. There was a hush over the entire administration building.

Little David was asleep on the wooden bench. Maria looked at Pablo sitting beside the smaller boy. And for the first time since he was a baby, she saw Pablo cry. He wept silently, the tears streaming down his face. She went to her brother and sat down next to him.

"Don't be afraid," she said. "Little bird, don't cry," she said as Aunt Carmen's face pictured itself in her mind.

Pablo looked up at Maria. Then he let his head drop on her shoulder and she put her arms around him.

Maria began to sing, first softly, then clearly and sweetly:

> Little bird, be still,
> Little bird, you will,
> Soon be winging away . . .
> Little bird, don't cry,
> Little bird, you'll fly,
> Tomorrow's another day . . .

The door opened and a policeman peered in. He smiled, and leaving the door open, tipped his chair against the wall.

96

Maria's lilting voice filled the room, hauntingly, beautifully:

> Little bird, you're young,
> You will fly among,
> Eagles soaring on high,
> You will grow up strong,
> Then she'll come along,
> And now away you will fly . . .

Pablo lifted his head and wiped his face with the back of his hands. He managed a faint smile.

> Little bird . . . little bird . . .

Pablo looked toward the door. He nudged his sister. The policeman was dozing. Maria sang chorus after chorus.

> Little bird, be still,
> Little bird, you will . . .

The policeman began to snore loudly. Maria dropped her voice and continued to sing. Pablo crept quietly to the door.

> . . . Soon be winging away . . .
> Little bird don't cry,
> Little bird, you'll fly . . .

Pablo motioned for Maria to come. Still singing, she gently awakened Little David and put her fingers to her lips. The boy sat up, saw the open door, and smiled broadly.

> Tomorrow's another day,
> Little bird you're young . . .

Maria and Little David joined Pablo at the door. They stepped out and looked down the hall. There was no one in sight. Everyone was having *siesta*. The three children moved quietly past the sleeping guard.

> You will fly among,
> Eagles soaring on high . . .

The kids stole down the hall as Maria's voice dropped to a hum. But the words of the song burst forth loudly in her head as they came to the main door.

> You will grow up strong,
> Then she'll come along,
> And now away you will fly . . .

Pablo opened the heavy door, and the three children ran out into the late-afternoon sun, free once more.

14

The sun had set and the *St. Agnes* was sailing toward San Diego. They had all had a silent supper together in the galley, then Ronnie went to his cabin. Jim came into Ronnie's cabin, and sat stiffly on the bunk opposite his son. Noches and Bandido were on the floor between them.

"All right," said Jim. "If you've got an explanation, I want to hear it."

"It wasn't right . . . dumping those kids like that," said Ronnie.

"We're not talking about what I did; we're talking about what you did. Jumping ship . . . causing damage. Why? That's what I want to know."

"I thought I could help them . . . get them back to San Diego."

"Spite!" said Jim. "You wanted to spite me. Admit it."

"No, I wanted to help . . ."

"You don't give a hoot for those kids! You wanted to make trouble for me! Didn't you? Answer me! Didn't you?"

"That's not it!" said Ronnie. "You're wrong! It was wrong to hand those kids over to the authorities!"

"Right or wrong, it was my decision!"

"You had no right . . ." said Ronnie.

"I had every right!" snapped Jim.

"You just wanted to get rid of them! Like you want to get rid of me!"

"What are you talking about?" shouted Jim.

"You'll dump me, too. I know you will . . . soon as you can!"

"That's not true," Jim said.

Ronnie was crying now, and he didn't care if his father saw him or not. "You never wanted me! You want to get rid of me! *That's* why I ran away . . . save you the trouble of dumping me! You never . . ."

Jim stood up, grabbed Ronnie by the shoulders, and raised him to his feet. "You're hysterical! Calm down!"

"You wouldn't care if you never saw me again! Well, I don't care either! I don't care . . . I don't . . ."

Stung by his son's words, and angry beyond reason, Jim shook Ronnie until he was silent. Then Ronnie pulled out of Jim's grasp, and the two stood looking at each other, their eyes locked in cold anger.

The ship suddenly lurched, sending Ronnie flying back onto his bunk. At the same time, the three box kids, in a tangle of arms and legs, slid out from under the opposite bunk. Both Ronnie and Jim stared at them in astonishment.

"I don't believe it!" gasped Jim.

Palbo tipped his cap and grinned sheepishly up at Jim. *"Buenas noches, señor,"* he said.

The ship heeled, and the door swung open. They heard Red's voice call. "Jim, we're heading into a squall!"

Jim turned and headed out the door. Then he looked back as if to make certain that the kids were not just a bad dream, after all.

The sound of the wind rose like a howling dog.

"Jim!" called Red urgently. "Get a move on!"

Jim slammed the door shut behind him.

Bandido yipped happily as he bounced around covering Pablo with wet kisses. Little David hugged Noches to his breast, then went to Ronnie and took his hand. "We're back," he said.

"But how . . . when . . ." Ronnie stuttered.

Pablo stood up and shouted above the wind. "We borrowed a rowboat! Came aboard while you were having supper in the galley!"

"We had to do it, Ronnie," Maria said. "Everybody in town knows about us. We'd be picked up. We thought you could keep us hidden until we got to San Diego."

The kids could hardly keep their footing as the ship rolled and shook with shuddering violence.

Ronnie put Little David on the bunk and sat down beside him; Maria and Pablo struggled to get to the bunk opposite. The boat pitched like a frenzied bronco. Bandido set up a howl, and Noches flew out of Little David's arms and circled the room in a panic.

Another wild rocketing of the ship sent Pablo and Maria onto the floor, as the door swung open. Maria scrambled to her feet and reached into the pocket of her sweater. Horrified, she pulled out the clay Madonna. The head was broken off at the neck. *"Jesús Maria!"* she breathed.

"The Madonna!" said Ronnie, coming to her side and taking the pieces of the statue.

"Por Dios!" said Pablo, crossing himself.

Then the three held onto each other as the ship rode into a deep wave.

Ronnie held the Madonna out to Maria. She shook her head and turned away. "A bad omen," she said. "We'll go to the *reformatório*. It's God's will." The boy put the broken statue on his bunk.

The swinging door banged loudly, and the three turned. Noches and Little David were nowhere to be seen.

"Little David!" said Ronnie. "He's gone!"

The three children wove their way through the main salon, the chart room, and the galley. Then they saw the boy standing on the top step of the companionway, the hatch open above him.

"Little David!" shouted Maria. "Come down!"

"Noches!" Little David yelled. "Noches is . . ." Then his words were swallowed up by the screaming wind, and he disappeared onto the open deck.

Ronnie was first to reach the hatch. He stepped onto the deck and held onto the coach roof to keep his footing. Maria and Pablo stood on the top step of the companionway and looked out.

Little David, oblivious to the fury of the wind and rain, was gazing up at the mainmast. Beyond him, Red was painfully picking his way up the shrouds. And above Red, perched on the spreaders, was Noches. Flapping his wings crazily and cackling at the top of his lungs, Noches was trying to untangle his claws from the rigging.

Another roll of the ship, and Little David was flattened on the deck.

"Get him!" shouted Maria to Ronnie. "Get Little David!"

On his hands and knees, Ronnie made his way to the little boy, and dragged him to the side of the cabin. But the boat pitched again, and they both slid back to the mast.

Maria and Pablo came onto the deck. The rain stung their faces and nearly blinded them.

"You kids! Get below!" Jim's voice came from the helm.

But the children's eyes were glued to the mast where Red was trying to grab hold of Noches. Suddenly, the bird, crazed with fright, struck out at Red's hand with his beak. Red yelled, drew back his hand, and began to slip down the mast. The ship dove into a deep, yawning well, and Red was thrown, with a sickening thud, down onto the deck, landing on his arm.

Maria screamed and put her hands over her eyes. When she looked again, Jim, Ronnie, and Pablo were kneeling beside Red. She moved closer.

"It's okay . . . I'm okay," said Red.

"Let's have a look," said Jim. He tore Red's sleeve to the elbow and felt the man's arm. "It's not broken."

"Nothing," Red said.

"Could be a torn ligament. You go below. I'm in charge now." Red started to protest. "That's an order!" Jim said.

Then Jim looked up at the rigging and mumbled under his breath. They all followed his gaze.

Noches was still trapped by the rigging. Several feet below, Little David, with all his might, was trying to make it up to the spreaders to rescue Noches.

"Come down!" shouted Maria. "Little David, come down!"

But the boy seemed not to hear as he continued up the mast. One by one, Little David untangled Noches's claws from the rigging. Then he put the bird under one arm. Now he looked down—and froze. He sat there, the rooster under one arm, holding onto the mast with the other.

The ship heaved as though out of control. "Help!" cried Little David. "I can't get down!"

"Go get him!" Jim said to Ronnie. "I've got to take the helm!"

Ronnie looked at his father as the man moved to the cockpit, then he looked at Red. "There's nobody else," said Red quietly.

104

Ronnie stared up at Little David. The spreaders seemed as high as a steeple.

"Ronnie! Help me!" cried the boy.

Ronnie grasped the mast as the rain sheeted down a torrent of slanted needles. He started up the mast slowly, then climbed, inch by inch, step by step, moving ever closer to Little David.

The highest wave Maria had ever seen was rolling swiftly toward the ship. The boat rode the wave up like a roller coaster, then seemed to hesitate a moment before the downward plunge. The ship, the wave, the people, all seemed to be suspended; all holding their breath at the same time.

Ronnie looked down into the bottomless canyon of the wave. He stiffened and clung to the mast desperately. "Roneeee . . ." Little David screamed as the ship plummeted into the deep chasm of the wave.

The ship leveled itself, but Ronnie still clung to the mast, a look of sheer terror frozen on his face.

"Ronnie, move!" shouted Red.

But Ronnie was paralyzed with fear. His arms and legs seemed to be made of stone.

A sudden hush filled the air while the wind inhaled for its next big blast. Nobody spoke for a long moment, all eyes held on Ronnie.

Then: "Hey, rich kid, can't you move?" shouted Pablo. "Rich kid can't move!" he taunted.

Ronnie looked down at Pablo. His terrified face relaxed, and he broke into a wide grin. "Buzz off, weirdo!" he yelled back.

Then he continued to climb—up, up, up. The rain pelted down in furious gusts, but the boy kept his pace. Slowly, steadily, Ronnie put one arm over the other, inching his way up while the wind whipped and howled at him.

Maria crossed the fingers of one hand. Then she crossed the fingers of the other hand. "*Jesús*, Mary, and Joseph," she prayed to herself. "Help them."

At last Ronnie made it to the spreaders. "Don't be afraid!" he shouted to Little David above the gale. "Hold on to me!"

Little David grabbed Ronnie around the neck, still holding Noches with his other hand.

"Wrap your legs around me!" ordered Ronnie. The younger boy did as he was told. "Now hold on tight!"

"Come on, rich kid! Come on, rich kid!" shouted Pablo while Ronnie and Little David came slowly down the mast.

"You're almost there! Just a little farther!" yelled Red.

Ronnie had only a few more feet to go when he lost his grip and tumbled to the deck. Little David and Noches landed on top of him.

"*Ay, mi Dios!*" breathed Maria.

The boys sat up. Noches, between them, gave out with a loud, triumphant crow.

They were safe!

15

The *St. Agnes* was sailing smoothly before a fresh breeze across the calm waters—a limitless meadow of unbroken blue. The sea was like a sheet of glass reflecting the high, cloudless sky. But even on this bright and sunny morning, the brilliant sun and balmy air did nothing to lift the spirits of the unhappy children.

Maria sighed. They would soon be in San Diego. They would soon be turned over to the *authorities.* They would soon be taken to Tijuana. They would soon be in the *reformatório!*

Ronnie and Little David were sprawled on the coach roof, staring glumly into space. Pablo and Maria were sitting on the deck below with Bandido at their feet. Noches, back to his normal self, was perched on the life rail. The water lap-lapped softly against the boat like one of Aunt Carmen's gentle lullabies.

The low murmur of Red's voice could be heard

from below. He had been busy since early morning in the chart room on the ship-to-shore radio. His words were indistinct, but suddenly the children could hear his deep laughter. Again, there was the murmur of his voice. Then: "Jim!" called Red. "Will you come below for a minute?"

"Coming!" answered Jim. He left the cockpit and disappeared down the open hatch.

Maria closed her eyes. The sun was warm on her face. She felt drowsy as Jim's and Red's voices drifted up to her. At first, the voices rose and fell like little ripply waves, then there was happy laughter and words like, "Great! Fine! Good work!"

Jim came back to the cockpit. Through half-opened eyes, Maria watched him as he stood at the helm. He began to hum a merry little tune. "Ronnie was right," thought Maria. "There must be a stone where his heart ought to be."

Ronnie and Little David slid down to the deck and sat next to Maria and Pablo. "Something's going on," said Ronnie.

"What?" said Pablo.

"I don't know . . . something. All that laughing and talking on the radio."

"Maybe they called the *authorities* to meet us at the pier," said Pablo.

"I don't wanna go to the *'formatório*," said Little David. "I wanna stay with Ronnie."

"We'll be friends, no matter what," Ronnie said. "All of us, okay?"

"Okay," grinned Pablo.

"Okay," said Maria.

"Let's shake on it and take a solemn oath." Ronnie put his hand out. Little David put his hand on top of Ronnie's. Maria put her hand under Ronnie's, and Pablo put his hand on top of all of theirs.

"Four friends forever," said Ronnie gravely as they shook their hands up and down.

"Forever," said Maria.

"Right," said Pablo.

"Me, too," said Little David.

Ronnie put his hand in his pocket and pulled out the repaired Madonna. "I fixed it," he said gruffly as he handed the statue to Maria.

The two stared at each other until Ronnie looked away, embarrassed. Her tears welling up, Maria licked her lips and swallowed hard. "*Gracias*, Ronnie," she whispered.

Suddenly, the boom swung over as the *St. Agnes* changed her course.

The kids stood up, puzzled.

"What's going on?" said Pablo.

"I don't know," answered Ronnie. "But I'm going to find out."

Ronnie went to the cockpit, the others following him.

Jim was still humming his gay little tune. He turned to Ronnie. "What's on your mind?" he said.

"The ship . . . we've changed course," said Ronnie. "Where are we headed?"

"To tell the truth, I don't really know," said Jim smiling.

"We're not going to San Diego?" said Pablo.

"Not unless you think that's a good place to start looking for your papa."

The children looked at each other in bewilderment, then back at Jim.

"Red and I thought we might head for La Paz. Then, maybe search awhile at Puerto Vallarta . . . then cruise to Acapulco."

Jim turned his attention back to the wheel, as though the subject was closed.

The children stared at each other again. Then Maria nodded at Jim and pushed Ronnie forward.

"Dad?" Ronnie said.

"Yes, son?"

"You're not going to turn the kids in?"

"No."

"You're going to take them with us on the cruise?"

"Only if they want to come along."

Pablo took off his driver's cap and tossed it in the air. "EEEYOW!!!" he shouted in glee.

"Wow . . . cool!" yelled Ronnie.

"Cool!" said Little David.

"*Gracias a Dios!*" exclaimed Maria.

Jim turned back to the children. "Now, settle down. There's work to be done on a ship," he said sternly. But his eyes were smiling.

"Yes, sir, captain, *señor!*" said Pablo.

"Ronnie," said Jim.

"Yes, sir," said Ronnie.

"It'll be a while before Red's of much use around here."

"Yes, sir?"

"It takes *two* men to crew this ship." Jim took Ronnie's hand and led him into the cockpit. Ronnie smiled broadly. The other kids watched as Jim took Ronnie's hands in his own and guided them to the wheel. Then with the boy in the circle of his arms, and his hands still over Ronnie's, Jim helped the boy steer the ship.

"Dig in," said Red as he passed out the plates of fresh peach pie. "This is going to have to last you until breakfast."

Despite having his arm in a sling, Red had put together a hearty supper for the famished children. He sat down and joined the others. Between all of them, they polished off two pies and three pitchers of milk.

"Everybody on board this ship is going to learn how to do the other man's job," Red said, wiping his mouth with a napkin. He indicated his injured arm. "In case any of us are ever in sick bay."

"I wanna steer," said Little David. "I wanna learn to drive."

"First thing tomorrow. But tonight, we're going to learn something about communication . . . the ship-to-shore radio," said Red.

Jim looked at his watch. "It's time, Red," he said.

"Everybody into the chart room," Red ordered.

Red sat down at the chart table as the others clustered around him. The radio was on a shelf above the table. "First," he said, indicating a knob, "Little David, turn on the radio."

Little David, feeling very important, clicked on the radio.

"Now," said Red, "we wait for it to warm up." They waited for a few moments. "Pablo, turn on the transmitter . . . here."

Pablo turned on another switch. Then Red held the microphone in the palm of his hand and depressed the mike button. "This is W-K-one-two-four-eight calling W-H-four-nine-six-two. This is Whiskey Kilo one-two-four-eight . . . calling Attorney Lawrence Silver. W-K-one-two-four-eight calling W-H-four-nine-six-two, Attorney Lawrence Silver. Come in, please. Over." He released the transmitter button and waited.

The radio hummed and sputtered for a moment. Then, from the loudspeaker: "W-H-four-nine-six-two, Attorney Lawrence Silver here."

"Is she ready to talk?" said Red. "We're waiting."

"Right here and ready," came the voice from the loudspeaker.

"Put her on," said Red. He turned to Maria. "Somebody wants to talk to you."

"Me?" said Maria in surprise.

"You," said Red, getting up.

Maria sat down at the chart table and held the mike. "What shall I say?" she asked.

"How about 'hello,' " said Red.

"Hello," said Maria. "Hello . . . hello . . . this is Maria."

"Maria, my child! My little bird!" said the voice on the other end.

Maria's eyes widened. "Aunt Carmen! It's Aunt Carmen!"

"Aunt Carmen! How can that be?" said Pablo.

"Shh, let me hear," said Maria. "Oh, Aunt Carmen, is it really you?"

"It's me, little bird. And how is Pablo?"

"We're all right," said Maria excitedly. "But where are you? Are you still being held? What happened to you? We waited and waited for you. How long will they hold you? What . . ."

Maria could hear the lilt of Aunt Carmen's laughter. "Hold on, child," she said. "One question at a time. Your good friends, *Señor* Hannigan and *Señor* Norton, they sent their *abogados*, their lawyers, to see me. I am free . . . free!"

"But they said you smuggled someone across the border . . ."

"The lawyers say they can prove my innocence," said Aunt Carmen. "I will still have to go to court, but I am free." Aunt Carmen paused. Now her voice sounded full of tears. "We have good friends, my child. *You* have good friends."

"When will we see you? I've missed you so much, Aunt Carmen!"

"There are many things I must do. It would be better if we come together after your voyage."

"But, Aunt Carmen . . ."

"Hush, little bird. Listen. I will be waiting on the pier when you return. For you and for Pablo."

114

"But you will be alone."

"I will be in good hands. The lawyers are looking after me. Have a good journey, little one. I must go now. *Vaya con Dios* . . . go with God."

"*Adiós*, Aunt Carmen."

"*Adiós*, little bird."

Jim sat on the chair and took over the mike. "Did you look into that other matter, Lawrence?" he said.

"It looks good. Go ahead with your plans. We'll keep working on the legal angles," said the voice on the loudspeaker.

"Good," said Jim. "This is W-K-one-two-four-eight, off and clear."

Jim put the mike down, turned in the swivel chair, and looked at the others, who formed a half-circle around him. He put Little David on his lap. He spoke slowly, clearly, so that the boy would understand him. "Your mother can't be found," he said. "There's a good chance she has gone to another state."

"Will I go to the *'formatório*?"

Jim tousled the boy's hair. "No such thing," Jim said. "You'll stay with us. With Ronnie and me."

"I get to stay with Ronnie?"

"For a long, long time. Maybe forever. Would you like that?"

For a moment, Little David's face lit up, then his expression grew sober. He watched Maria's face as he spoke. "I don't know," he said haltingly. "I wanna be with Ronnie . . . but I wanna be with Maria and Pablo, too."

"You will be," said Jim. "All this summer and

maybe the next, too." He paused. "Who can tell how many summers it will take us to find their papa?"

Little David jumped off Jim's lap, ran to Ronnie, and threw his arms around the boy's waist. "Then I'll stay with Ronnie!" he shouted happily.

The children lay in their bunks, not even pretending to try to settle down.

"Ronnie?" said Little David.

"Yeah," answered Ronnie.

"I can't sleep."

"Try," said Ronnie.

"Can I come down and sleep with you?"

"Okay."

The little boy climbed off his bunk and slid in next to Ronnie. "Hey, rich kid," said Pablo.

"What do you want, weirdo?"

"I gotta do KP tomorrow . . . gotta help Red in the galley."

"Tough," said Ronnie.

"Think I'll do some fishing. Catch me a marlin."

"Huh!" scoffed Ronnie. "Be lucky if you catch a minnow. Now, me, I'm gonna get me a sailfish."

"Wanna bet?" said Pablo.

"Sure."

"Guy that gets the biggest fish does the KP, okay?"

"It's a bet," said Ronnie.

Maria lay thinking for a long time. And her thoughts buzzed in her mind like bees around a hive. No more worry about going to the *reformatório*. No.

more hiding from the *authorities*. No more wondering where Aunt Carmen was.

The creaking sounds of the ship lulled her into a warm, soft drowsiness, and she could tell by the sound of their breathing that the boys were all asleep. She sighed deeply, contentedly.

Then, quietly, Maria slipped out of her bunk and got down on her knees. "Thank you, God," she prayed. "Thank you for Jim and for Red and for Aunt Carmen and the lawyers. And bless Ronnie and Pablo and Little David and Noches and Bandido and me. Amen."

ABOUT THE AUTHOR

Anne Snyder is the author of numerous television scripts and magazine articles. She is also a teacher of creative writing for gifted children at Valley College in North Hollywood and a consultant to Open Space, Inc., an educational program funded by the federal government. Ms. Snyder is the author of the widely-praised *50,000 Names for Jeff*. She and her husband live in Van Nuys, California.

ABOUT THE ARTIST

Diane de Groat is a graduate of Pratt Institute. She has illustrated and designed many books for children, including *Truth and Consequences*, *A Book for Jodan*, *Luke Was There*, and *Four Seasons, Five Senses*. Ms. de Groat lives in Brooklyn, New York.

ABOUT THE BOOK

This book was set in Linotype Caledonia with display in Photo Typositor Burko Bold 2. The illustrations were done in charcoal.